"Are you going to answer me?"

Her pulse drummed underneath his fingertips.

"What can I tell you, Amber? Do you want to hear that I think you're beautiful? That you make me want things that I don't deserve? That I will never deserve? Because I'll say it. And then what? You'll feel sorry for me—"

Amber spun around with all that ire in her eyes that was so damn sexy. "I couldn't possibly feel sorry for you, Rylan."

This close, her body was flush with his and he could feel her breasts rising and falling when she spoke. He dropped his hands, looping his arms around her waist. All he could feel right then was the desire sweeping through him, consuming him with need.

"All I can feel is the same thing you do."

Looking into her glittery eyes wasn't helping his situation any. "This is a bad idea," he said.

Amber looked up at him and locked on to his gaze.

"A storm never stopped me, Rylan."

WHAT SHE KNEW

USA TODAY Bestselling Author

BARB HAN

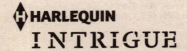

HARLEQUIN
INTRIGUE

All my love to Brandon, Jacob and Tori,
the three great loves of my life.

To Babe, my hero, for being my greatest love and
my place to call home.

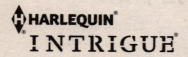

ISBN-13: 978-1-335-13647-3

What She Knew

Copyright © 2020 by Barb Han

Recycling programs
for this product may
not exist in your area.

This edition published by arrangement with Harlequin Books S.A.

For questions and comments about the quality of this book, please contact us at CustomerService@Harlequin.com.

Harlequin Enterprises ULC
22 Adelaide St. West, 40th Floor
Toronto, Ontario M5H 4E3, Canada
www.Harlequin.com

Printed in U.S.A.

USA TODAY bestselling author **Barb Han** lives in north Texas with her very own hero-worthy husband, three beautiful children, a spunky golden retriever/standard poodle mix and too many books in her to-read pile. In her downtime, she plays video games and spends much of her time on or around a basketball court. She loves interacting with readers and is grateful for their support. You can reach her at barbhan.com.

Books by Barb Han

Harlequin Intrigue

Rushing Creek Crime Spree

Cornered at Christmas
Ransom at Christmas
Ambushed at Christmas
What She Did
What She Knew

Crisis: Cattle Barge

Sudden Setup
Endangered Heiress
Texas Grit
Kidnapped at Christmas
Murder and Mistletoe
Bulletproof Christmas

Cattlemen Crime Club

Stockyard Snatching
Delivering Justice
One Tough Texan
Texas-Sized Trouble
Texas Witness
Texas Showdown

Harlequin Intrigue Noir

Atomic Beauty

Visit the Author Profile page at Harlequin.com.

CAST OF CHARACTERS

Amber Kent—This Kent family ranch heiress puts her life on the line to help an old friend, but her heart is out of range.

Rylan Anderson—This former SEAL's infant daughter is a game changer in more ways than one.

Brooklyn Anderson—This little girl brings trouble to town on her heels.

Teague Thompson—The lawyer who swears Brooklyn's adoption is legit.

Veronica Robinson—This woman is desperate—but just how far will she go?

Cornell Robinson—This man is used to getting what he wants, no matter the cost.

Chapter One

Amber Kent didn't normally pick up calls from numbers she didn't recognize on her personal cell. She tapped her toe on the floorboard while waiting for Harvey Baily to finish loading hay bales onto her truck. He'd insisted she stay in the cab in order to keep warm.

The temperature hovered just above forty degrees. The sun was covered by thick gray clouds. She stared at her buzzing phone. The call could be coming from a distant relative. She'd had a few of those since losing her parents a few years ago. It was past the holidays.

Glancing in the rearview mirror, she noticed that Harvey wasn't even close to being done loading. She had a couple of minutes to spare.

"Hello," she said. The silence on the other end had her thinking answering was a bad idea.

"Amber, this is Rylan Anderson…" The familiar voice came through the line clearly. He didn't need to say his name for her to know that voice. It was deeper now, but that unmistakable timbre goose bumped her arms. Talk about a blast from the past. How long had it been? Eight years? Nine?

"I heard you moved back to town, but I thought people were pulling my leg." After nearly a decade of being gone, she was surprised he'd come back to Jacobstown, Texas.

"Yeah, sorry I didn't get in touch." That was an odd thing to say. Had he planned on seeing her at some point?

"It's fine," she said quickly. Too quickly?

"I know it's been a long time but I need a favor." At least he didn't pretend this was a social call. So why did disappointment wrap around her? A little piece of her wished he was calling to see how she was, or if she wanted to meet up for coffee. Hearing from him after all these years was a shock to the system.

"What can I do for you?" she asked, suppressing a small sigh.

She heard something *or someone* in the background. Then again, it could be a TV. She couldn't make out the noise clearly.

"I didn't have anyone else to call who could handle..." His voice trailed off, and that really got her curiosity going. He didn't sound like himself. Although, what did she expect? He'd gone dim on social media after leaving Jacobstown to join the military. Platforms had changed, phone numbers had changed and she didn't keep up with him.

"What is it?" she asked. Curiosity was getting the best of her. What on earth could make him call after all this time?

"It's hard to explain. Can you stop by my house?"

"Um, sure." She didn't have a clue about why. "Are you in some kind of trouble?"

"Yeah. Kind of," he hedged. "I don't know—"

"The bank's closed if you need mon—"

"It's not like that." There was a hint of defensiveness in his voice that she hadn't meant to put there. "You know what? Never mind. This is a mistake."

"Hold on, Rylan—"

It was too late. He'd ended the call.

Amber wasn't letting him get away with that. She called him back.

He picked up on the first ring. The noise in the background confused her. "Where are you? What's going on?"

He issued a sharp sigh.

"Rylan, I can drop by. Don't be a mule," she said.

There was a long pause. "I'd really appreciate it."

He sounded like someone with a migraine coming on, and for a split second she wondered if he needed medical attention.

"You're okay, right? I mean, you're not injured,"

she said, and she didn't bother hiding the worry in her tone.

"It's not like that." At least she'd ruled out a trip to the ER.

"Text your address and I'll stop by on my way home." She should probably turn and drive in the opposite direction from her brother's former best friend. The trouble was that she'd counted Rylan as a friend once, too. Plus, it was just beyond the holiday season. Rumors that he'd moved back to town were true. And he shouldn't be on his own. How could she refuse his plea for help? The text came through immediately after the call ended. She knew exactly where that was. Mrs. Parker used to live there, and Amber had stopped by many times to drop off a meal before the widow moved away.

Harvey tapped on Amber's truck bed as he closed the tailgate. He waved. His job was done. She rolled down the driver's side window and shouted a thank-you through the howling wind. A chill settled over her, and she realized the temperature had dropped another ten degrees. It was going to be a cold night if the rest of that front moved through town.

Jacobstown was an hour's drive south of Fort Worth. It was considered a bedroom community that had been a safe haven until recent weeks when some twisted individual started mutilating the left hooves of animals. The perp had started with small animals and then worked his way up to heifers. Several had been found on the Kent Ranch, a place she owned with five brothers.

Amber navigated onto Main Street and across town to Mrs. Parker's old house. It was Saturday, and there weren't many vehicles on the roads. She imagined grocery stores were probably busy with everyone anticipating the weather. She tapped her right thumb against the steering wheel. There was something about the tone of Rylan's voice that wasn't sitting right. Her first thought was that she should've asked him to come to the ranch. But she was close enough to stop by his house on her way home from the feed store, and she figured part of the reason he hadn't contacted her yet was because of the blowout he'd had with her brother Will. Eight years was a long time to hold on to a grudge. It wasn't like Will to do that, either.

Whatever had transpired between the two of them was kept quiet, no small feat for a town that seemed to know everyone's business in real time. People weren't nosy. They cared. Ranch families had a long history of looking out for one another.

Fifteen minutes later Amber pulled up in front of Rylan's bungalow-style house and parked. At least the place wasn't on fire. She'd worried his emergency was something like that based on the urgency in his voice, but she also realized he'd be calling the fire department and not her.

Her curiosity had her mind running through half a dozen wild scenarios before she'd arrived. Last she'd heard, Rylan was a Navy SEAL. There probably wasn't much that he couldn't handle on his own. Needing her made even less sense as she rolled over possible problems in her head.

By most accounts Rylan had been in Jacobstown for two weeks already, and she had yet to see him. He'd basically pushed her out of his life before he'd signed up with the military eight years ago. He'd walked away without looking back not long after the one kiss they'd shared, but this wasn't the time to rehash that memory. Besides, he probably didn't even remember it.

Amber hopped out of the truck, took a deep breath and moved to the front door. There were ten-gallon buckets of paint littering the covered porch. Paint chipped off the outside of the building. She stepped over a ladder in order to get to the front door.

Rylan didn't seem to expect any visitors. She knocked, and it felt like it took forever for him to answer. It didn't. She had a case of nerves. She'd tried to shake them off before seeing him again and clearly hadn't.

"Thanks for coming, Amber." Rylan opened the door for a peek, blocking her view into his home. He looked a little too good in what she could see of his jeans and long-sleeve T-shirt. Her heart performed an inappropriate little flip-flop routine at seeing him again. She didn't want to have those feelings for him, like the childhood crush she'd had. She was an adult now, and there was no room in her life for childish pursuits.

Rylan's dark curls had been clipped off, but that did nothing to take away from his good looks. The military had filled him out even more, and she had to force her eyes away from his chest, which had always been at eye level.

"You're welcome." She tried to look past him and see what he was blocking. "What's going on, Rylan? I don't hear from you in eight or nine—"

"Eight," he interjected.

"Fine, eight years it's been, and now I get an emergency call from you out of the blue? I don't see your house burning down, and you're not letting me inside. I'm a little confused as to why I'm here."

"Damn." He muttered something else under his breath that she couldn't make out. "This is harder than I thought."

"What is it, Rylan? Why did you call me?" Impatience had her tapping the toe of her boot on his concrete porch.

"Did you buy this place?" She hoped Mrs. Parker

was okay. She'd moved six months ago to be closer to her daughter in San Antonio.

"I'm in the process," he said, and an emotion she couldn't quite pinpoint darkened his eyes.

"It's good to see you, Amber." He closed the door a little tighter against his side. He was massive at six foot three inches. He'd always been tall, but now he was filled out, too. It made a huge difference in his size and aided his ability to completely block her view.

Amber planted a balled fist on her hip, ignoring the reaction her body was having at seeing him again. "What's so important that my hay had to wait?"

A baby let out a wail.

"Come on in and see for yourself." He looked at her with the most helpless expression.

"What have you done, Rylan Anderson?" Amber stomped through the doorway and froze. Her jaw must've dropped. Rylan stared at her, but all she could focus on was the baby on the floor, lying on a blanket with couch pillows tucked all around her. "Is this yours?"

"I don't know," he admitted.

"What do you mean by that?" Okay, she understood what he was saying, but it was more like a *seriously? How could this happen? And how could you not know if this is your child?*

"A random person showed up at my door with her." Rylan looked helplessly at the little girl who'd settled back down already. He really did sound lost and confused. His dark eyes had that lost quality, too.

"Where's her mother?" Amber scanned the place. Her blood boiled that a person could drop a baby off and run like that.

"That's a great question." His voice held a mixture of frustration and desperation.

Thankfully, the baby had gone back to sleep.

"How did this happen?" She walked over and stood near the little pink bundle. She was young, a few months old if Amber had to guess. She'd been around her brothers' children enough to know a little bit about babies.

Looking down at that sleeping angel caused Amber's heart to squeeze. The air thinned, and it became difficult to breathe. She would never be able to look at such a young baby without remembering her loss. She reminded herself that it was a long time ago. And she still couldn't go there, couldn't allow her thoughts to run rogue without the world trying to crash down around her. She refocused on her former friend.

Rylan stood there, looking at a loss for words and staring at her like she had three foreheads.

"Okay, fine. I'm not that naive. I know *how* this happened. I'm just wondering…never mind…you got coffee?" She figured she was going to need some serious caffeine if she was going to think straight. She shook off the cold and shrugged out of her coat, which he immediately took from her and tossed onto the chair near the door.

"I put on a pot." He turned toward the kitchen. "Here, let me—"

"No, thanks. You stay in here in case she wakes up again." Amber didn't want to explain the sudden burst of emotion that made tears well in her eyes. She knew better than to let Rylan see them, or he'd have too many questions. She stalked past him and into the adjacent kitchen.

She opened a couple of cabinets before she found the right cupboard. The coffeemaker was near the sink and easy to spot. There were unpacked boxes stacked against the wall in one corner. "You want a cup?"

"Yes. Please."

Amber wiped her eyes and straightened her back before filling the mugs she'd taken from the cupboard and returning to the living room with two steaming coffees.

"Here you go." She handed one to him and then took a sip of hers, enjoying the burn. She needed to clear a few cobwebs in order to think clearly. She plopped down on the floor, near the baby.

"Come join me, Rylan," she said.

He did.

"You've been in some messes before, Rylan Anderson, but I can't even begin with this one." She took another sip and lowered her voice. "You don't know if you're the father?"

"This is the first time I've set eyes on her," he admitted. "I had no clue that she existed until someone knocked on my door looking panicked, asked me to hold her and then ran. She was crying, and I had no idea what to do. The person said her mother asked him to drop the child off. He also said I'm her father, apologized and was gone before I could stop him."

Amber looked down at the sleeping baby. She had Rylan's dark curls, which didn't exactly mean she belonged to him. She just looked like she *could* be his daughter. The thought of Rylan being a daddy hit her hard in the chest.

"Okay. Here's what we'll do. You can get a DNA test down at the store. I think they're pretty easy to take. If she's yours, we'll take the next legal steps for you to claim her." Her statement didn't get the reaction she was hoping for.

"How accurate can a drugstore test be?" Rylan looked even more lost. "I need to track down her mother, and I can't do that if I don't know who she is."

"How many women have you been with?" Before he could answer, she held up a hand. "Don't answer that. It's not my business."

"This situation is complicated, Amber. But I'm not some jerk who runs around getting women pregnant and then ditching them. I just got out of the military and, yes, there've been a few women, but none who were important, and I'm *always* careful." The indignation in his voice shouldn't make her want to smile. Rylan would be considered hot by pretty much any woman with eyes. He was also smart and funny.

"I'm not trying to judge you unfairly, Rylan. I'm really not." It was a mistake to look into his dark brown eyes while sitting this close.

He looked away and took a sip of coffee. "It doesn't matter. She's here and I have no idea who she is, where she came from, or if she's mine. But I can't help wondering who would track me down and play a twisted prank like this, either."

"Did you say the stranger dropped off a diaper bag?" She was already looking around for one.

The living room had a sofa, chair and boxes. On the opposite wall was a perfectly set up and organized flat screen. There were two-by-two-inch swatches of paint colors taped to the wall that got the most natural light.

"It's over there." He pointed next to the sofa.

"Did you check it for a name?" she asked.

He shook his head.

Amber retrieved it and opened the zipper compartments one by one. She blew out a breath. "I don't see anything."

She held up the bag. A name was embroidered on the front pocket in small letters. *Brooklyn.* She showed it to Rylan. "The bag might've been borrowed, but we can call her Brooklyn for now."

"It's a start," he agreed.

"What about social media? Surely, if you spent time with someone intimately you'd be following them or the other way around." Discussing Rylan's sex life wasn't high on her list of post-holiday musts. Jealousy took another jab at her, so she straightened her shoulders. A man as hot and charming as Rylan had sex with women, probably any women he wanted. It wasn't her place to judge. She'd had sex, too. She figured the only difference was that they were presently talking about *his* sex life.

"I'm not much on that computer stuff," he said, that lost look in his eyes returning. "But, Amber, wouldn't I know if I had a child?"

Chapter Two

Rylan didn't expect seeing Amber again to hit him like a physical blow. It did. All he'd known when he'd made the SOS call was that he was in way over his head and he needed a female perspective. His mind had immediately snapped to Amber. He'd tried to tell himself the reason was that he'd dated most of the women in Jacobstown, which wasn't much once high school was over, and that he figured Amber was safe. He nearly laughed out loud. Amber Kent safe.

The knockout youngest member of the Kent family could not be more fireworks and temptation. She was beautiful as ever. No, check that, she was even more beautiful than before. And that wasn't exactly good for Rylan's heart.

Her nutmeg-colored hair was in one of those thick French braids. A few strands broke free and fell beside her heart-shaped face, framing eyes that could best be described as a warm, light brown. She was the total package, full pink lips and creamy skin.

She stood at roughly five foot seven and had legs that went on for days. Her hips were curvier than he remembered, which only made her sexier. He knew better than to let those unproductive thoughts occupy his mind.

As much as he liked looking at a pretty face and a hot body, Amber was so much more. Her intelligence and sense of humor had been the first things he'd noticed about her. Well, after they'd both gotten over those awkward teen years. She'd come through it all so easily. Not him. He'd become angry and headed down a bad path with the wrong people, which had led to him shutting out his best friend. This wasn't the time to dive down that slippery slope of shame and regret.

"I'm drawing a blank on who the mother could be." Embarrassing as it was to admit, he had no clue. He had no excuses, either.

"This baby looks to be few months old. My best guess is around three," she stated.

"How do you know?" He had no clue.

"We've had a baby boom at the ranch." She shot him a look like she just realized he wasn't caught up on her family's life. "Don't ask."

He glanced at her ring finger. Relief he had no right to own washed over him when he saw no gold band. "Didn't plan to."

"Good. The mother would've been pregnant for nine months. So where were you…" She paused looking like she was making a mental calculation and counted on her fingers. "Twelve months ago, give or take?"

Rylan rubbed the scruff on his chin. He looked away from those distracting eyes. "There was a weekend that I don't remember much about. I must've had too much to drink."

"No one drinks so much that they can't remember where they were or who they were with, Rylan," she argued.

He thought back to where he might've been a year ago and drew a blank. "The thing is… I used to drink and that got me into a lot of trouble. I quit. Even when I drank, I never partied so much that I was careless enough to…" He motioned toward the baby.

"Well, that's good to know." She blew out a breath. "She's probably not even yours. This is most likely a mix-up."

Amber pulled out a piece of paper from the diaper bag. "I didn't see this before."

"What is it?"

"A note from someone. The mother?"

Guilt stabbed at Rylan. There was that one time he'd gone to a party and woke up the next day in a motel room, alone. A hazy memory said there was a woman with him that night. Everything was foggy, and it felt more like a dream than reality. He'd felt off for a few days afterward, most likely the effects of alcohol after not drinking anything stronger than a cup of coffee for years.

She skimmed the note. "It's not signed. But it's addressed to you, and the baby's name *is* Brooklyn."

Rylan thought back to that weekend. Was that twelve months ago? It seemed longer than that, which meant he couldn't be the father of the child. What would the odds be of those dates matching up? They had to be slim. "What else?"

Amber held up the piece of paper and shrugged. "That's it. At least we know her name for certain now."

Rylan studied Amber. She had that same lost look from when she first saw the baby.

"I need to call Zach." Rylan referred to the sheriff, who also happened to be Amber's cousin.

"What can he do?" she asked.

"I don't know. Call in Child Protective Services?" There was no conviction in his words. "Find this kid's mother?"

"And what if she is yours? Do you plan to ignore that fact, Rylan, because if you do I won't recognize you anymore." She was all anger and ire. Damn that she was even more beautiful when she was scolding him. He shouldn't find it amusing or cute as hell.

"I would never deny my own child." It was true. Rylan knew firsthand what it was like to have a father who couldn't be bothered with his child. When Rylan was young, his mother had told him that his father had gone camping. He later realized that she was covering for the fact that Rylan's father had walked out on them both. The man didn't look back. He just disappeared one day, leaving Rylan's mother to care for him long before Rylan had any memories of his father.

His mother had worked two, sometimes three jobs to pay the bills. He'd loved her and respected her, but he never knew her. Loralee Anderson was always gone, working, trying to make a living. When she became sick and passed away when Rylan was in high school, he had rebelled. He'd gotten out of control. And then the night he'll never forget happened. Even now, he couldn't go there mentally.

The US Navy had become his family once he decided to get his act together and join. Then, his brothers on his SEAL team were his only family. And yet he'd never quite been able to erase Jacobstown from his mind.

Now that his time was up in the military, and he'd had no designs on a forever career, Rylan came back to the only place he'd ever known as home. Except nothing was the same anymore. Strange how moving away from the place he grew up made him think it would somehow be frozen in time when he returned. It didn't work that way. Life moved on. People grew up and grew older.

"Are you listening?" Amber interrupted his heavy thoughts. She blinked at him.

"Yes. Sorry. What were you saying again?" He took another sip of coffee to wake up his mind. He'd stayed up too late last night unpacking the kitchen, but at least the place was close to livable now. He planned to move a wall in order to open up the living area to the kitchen. There were other renovations on deck. Once the place was updated, Rylan had planned to decide if it was worth sticking around Jacobstown.

"Where's your laptop?" Amber set her coffee on the table next to the couch.

"Ah, over here." He retrieved it and sat next to her.

She opened it and asked him to log into his social media page. She looked at his story and skimmed all the people—mostly women—who followed him.

He could've sworn she'd blown out a frustrated breath.

"There are a lot of names here, Rylan." She studied the screen.

"Yeah, I know a lot of people thanks to traveling all over the world," he said.

"Thank you for your service," she said, and there was a hint of admiration in her voice. It made him proud to hear it.

"You're welcome," he said reflexively. He'd heard it dozens of times over the years, but it sounded somehow sweeter coming from Amber. He told himself that he couldn't afford to care about what she really thought of him, even though a little voice in the back of his head called him out on the lie.

"Okay." She refocused on the screen. "Let's get to work on these names."

She pulled up picture after picture, but he didn't remember being with any of the faces. Especially not in the time frame that would be necessary for one of them to be the mother of the child.

"It's no good." He was getting frustrated.

"We'll figure it out," Amber reassured him.

It was easy for her to say. Everything in life came easy to Amber Kent. Beauty? Check. Brains? Check. Great family who loved her? Check. Money? Check.

"Everything can't be fixed by the Kent charm." He nudged her shoulder with his. A surprising amount of electricity pulsed from where they made contact. Well, that was a bad idea. One Rylan had no intention of repeating.

His attraction to Amber came roaring back, but he remembered the promise he'd made to his best friend. Will Kent knew Rylan better than anyone else, and if Will thought Rylan dating Amber was a bad idea, then it was. Period.

Besides, Rylan would never break a promise to his former best friend.

"Ha-ha. Very funny. You know, luck visits those

wearing overalls more often than someone who can't be bothered to get his hands in the dirt," she shot back.

"True." He picked up her hand and showed off her manicured nails.

"Just because I know how to clean up doesn't mean I don't put in the work, Rylan Anderson." Hearing his name roll off her tongue shouldn't sound so good. He should also ignore the electricity bouncing between them. Those were things that had gotten him into trouble before, and he'd touched the hot stove once.

Rylan liked to think that he learned from his mistakes.

The baby stirred. Rylan had never been around kids and he hoped, no prayed, the little thing wouldn't wake before someone from CPS could get here. He had no idea what to do with a baby, and was grateful that Amber had shown up before the little girl woke and started crying again. Her wails had damn near broken his heart before she tuckered herself out and fell asleep.

Rylan had never felt so useless or helpless in his life. He'd practically worn a path in the carpet making circles in the living room as he held her against his chest. It was the only position she seemed remotely soothed in.

"I know you work hard," he conceded. "I also know that you're smarter than me. So, what do I do with this?" He motioned toward the black-haired angel. "Because I'm out of my league here. I surrender."

"Like you said, we can start by calling Zach. You know my cousin will come right over. News will get out, too. News that you're possibly a daddy. News that I was here." She flashed eyes at him, and he realized she was asking if he was prepared for her brother to know she was at his place. "Are you prepared for her to be tied up in the system until the courts figure out paternity?"

He hadn't thought of it that way. He'd been too focused on trying to ensure he wasn't left alone with her for long. He didn't have the first clue how to care for a baby. But Amber made a good point, and it was something he needed to seriously consider.

"No. If she's mine, then I want her with me. I'd also like to figure out who her mother is either way. I mean, having this dropped on my doorstep has rocked my world, and I want to know if this is a babysitting detail or if some person is going to show up in six months with a court order demanding her baby back."

He didn't do the unknown real well, especially with stakes this high.

Chapter Three

Amber's cousin, Zach McWilliams, happened to be nearby when she called to explain Rylan's situation. The sheriff was on his way over. Questions were mounting, and Rylan needed answers. He could hardly imagine that a person could abandon such a sweet child. Even when Brooklyn had cried in his arms earlier she'd done it softly.

There was something delicate and tiny about the little girl that brought out Rylan's protective instincts. She had the roundest cheeks, the thickest head of curly hair and the most angelic features he'd ever seen.

Granted, Rylan hadn't been much on babies before, and had no intention of having one of his own until he had something to offer. That was one of many reasons he hoped this one had a different father. But as far as babies went, he'd be lucky to have one like her.

A soft knock sounded at the door, and Rylan immediately walked over and let Zach in.

"Thanks for coming on such short notice," Rylan said.

"Good to see you again." Zach's wary expression made sense given the circumstances. All Amber had told her cousin was that she needed to speak to him at Rylan's house, and that she'd explain everything when Zach arrived.

His gaze bounced from Amber to the sleeping baby to Rylan. Amber gave her cousin a hug. He eyed the stacks of unpacked boxes.

"I'm still getting settled," Rylan said by way of explanation.

"I heard you were back," Zach said. "Welcome home."

Rylan thanked him. He hadn't been sure of the reception he'd get from anyone connected to the Kent family. But then it wasn't like Will Kent to go spreading rumors.

Amber motioned toward the couch. "Sit down."

"I'm good." Zach stood in an athletic stance like he was preparing himself for just about anything. He looked to Rylan. "What's going on?"

"A guy shows up at my door. He's holding a baby in a carrier and has a diaper bag on his shoulder. I just moved in so I figure he has the wrong address or is looking to visit Mrs. Parker, who used to own this place."

"She moved to San Antonio to be close to her daughter," Zach confirmed. He'd pulled out a notebook and pencil. He looked up from the notes he was scribbling.

"Yeah. The place had been empty and she needed the money. I figured we'd both win if I bought it," Rylan said.

"So, you're planning on sticking around?" Zach asked.

Rylan glanced at Amber before returning his gaze to Zach. "That's the idea for now. I figure I can always rent the place out if I decide to move to the city."

"People need affordable housing." Zach was nodding. "The guy who showed up. Had you ever seen him before that you can recall?"

"First time," Rylan said. "He shows up and asks if I'm Rylan Anderson. I tell him yes and then his cell goes off. It wakes the baby and she starts crying. He looks flustered, asks me if I can hold the baby carrier while he answers his phone. The minute I take the carrier he drops the diaper bag at my feet, tells me the kid is mine and then bolts."

"Did you chase him?" Zach asked.

"By the time I set the baby down and kicked the bag out of the way, he had too much of a head start.

She was crying, sounding pitiful, so I didn't have it in my heart to leave her. I looked up, but by then the guy disappeared in between the neighbors' houses." Rylan was still annoyed that he'd been outplayed.

"What did he look like?" Zach jotted down notes.

"He was around five feet nine inches. He had blond hair and blue eyes. He was young. I'd say in his early twenties. He was slim, looked like a runner. He had thin features," Rylan stated.

"Think you could work with a sketch artist?" Zach asked.

Rylan nodded as the little girl stirred. She immediately started winding up to cry. Again, Rylan felt useless. He looked toward Amber.

"She's probably hungry," Amber said, picking the baby up like it was as natural as a Sunday walk. Bouncing the little girl kept her from wailing. "You two keep talking. I'll figure out how to make her a bottle. Do you have a microwave?"

"Yes," Rylan said. He turned his attention back to Zach as Amber disappeared.

The baby cried louder once in the kitchen, and he figured Amber had her hands full. She probably needed help.

Rylan followed the sound. "What do you want me to do?" He had to do something. He couldn't stand helplessly by and watch Amber do all the work. He wasn't a jerk.

Zach waited with the patience of a Sunday-school teacher in church.

Amber mixed a packet of formula with bottled water that she'd heated. She filled the bottle and secured the lid. The little girl latched on and then settled in Amber's arms. Rylan didn't want to notice how natural Amber looked holding a baby. *His baby?*

"I have no idea if the child is mine. There was one time I was with someone, but I'm not even sure the dates match up," Rylan admitted.

Zach asked a few routine-sounding questions that Rylan didn't know the answers to.

"What happens now, Zach?" Rylan needed to know what was going to happen to the little girl.

"This is where we call in Child Protect—"

"Let's say that wasn't an option," Rylan interrupted. "What then?"

Amber's gaze darted from the little girl in her arms to Rylan and back.

"A case could be made for her to stay with a parent," Zach informed him.

"We haven't established paternity." Rylan had no idea if he was the little girl's father, but no kid deserved to be dropped off and left behind. Being rejected by the two people who were supposed to love a kid the most made for a bad upbringing. Although Rylan was never a bad kid, per se, he'd managed his fair share of trouble over the years, especially in high school.

Thinking about restitution for the trouble he'd caused the Willow family was a large part of the reason he'd moved back to town. He owed them and had every intention of making good.

"I'll make that call and see who's available at CPS," Zach said. "Before you tell me you don't have to meet the CPS worker and that you have a comfort level with the child, I'll make that call to see who's available. The other option is to let her stay here."

Rylan looked at the little girl, who seemed content to curl up in Amber's arms. "I'll meet the person you send."

Brooklyn Anderson? He did like how that sounded.

Zach excused himself to make a call. He returned a minute later. "Elise Shelton is on her way."

"What will happen to her?" Rylan motioned toward Brooklyn.

"She'll be placed in a temporary home until her identity can be established via a DNA test and her parents are located," Zach informed him.

Rylan appreciated Zach for not automatically assuming she belonged to him. If she turned out to be his daughter, he would figure out a way to make her feel at home in his house, in *their* home.

"Any chance I can keep her here until this mess is sorted out?" Rylan didn't have a legal leg to stand on. Maybe there was a loophole? If not, he'd have to rely on Zach's good nature.

The sheriff's eyebrows shot up in surprise. "You would want to do that? Don't get me wrong, it's a noble gesture but babies need a lot of care. Do you know how to make a bottle or change a diaper?"

Rylan shrugged. "I wouldn't sign up for it voluntarily but here she is. Being dropped off here must've been traumatic for her, and the thought of sending her off to someone and changing her environment again doesn't sit right. And here's the thing, what if she *is* my child? Then what? She gets bounced back here right where we started?"

"I see your point." Zach's expression was calm, serious. "What if she's not your child? What if a mother is running away from someone? What if she picked your name off a mailbox and found a random person to tell you this story?"

"That's all the more reason for me to keep her. I can protect her." Rylan was dead serious about that. His military training made him the best qualified to handle a threat, foreign or domestic.

"Do you know how to care for a baby?" Zach asked again. "Don't take this the wrong way, but they're a handful."

Rylan needed to think long and hard about his next move.

"I'll stick around and help with the baby until her paternity gets sorted out," Amber volunteered.

Zach's gaze flew to her. She shrugged, trying to dismiss the innuendo that she was offering for another reason, like she was attracted to Rylan.

"You sure that's such a good idea?" Zach asked.

"I'm not going to turn my back on a friend, Zach. Besides, he's never taken care of a baby before as far as I know, and you just pointed out what a handful one could be." Throwing his own words back at him usually worked in disagreements with her cousin. She knew he had her best interests at heart, but she also knew her own mind. "Do you really want this sweet little girl bounced around? And, as Rylan said, there's a chance you'll be bringing her right back here at the end of a couple of days anyway."

Zach stood there, staring at the carpet. She knew she was getting through to him.

"I doubt this will take long to decipher, and then I'll be back at the ranch doing my own thing again," she added for good measure.

"What if the DNA test reveals that Rylan is the father?" Zach was tapping his toe. "What then?"

"He'll have to figure out his next moves when that time comes," Amber admitted. "Until then, I plan to give him a hand."

Rylan would have to hire help. There were a few grandmothers in Jacobstown who had free time on their hands and who wouldn't mind a babysitting job. Amber could think of three off the top of her head, and she'd be happy to supply names. Heck, at least one of them would babysit for free just to have something to do. Granted, individually they couldn't handle Brooklyn all day by themselves, but something could be worked out.

"Your heart's in the right place, Amber. It is," Zach started. "But you have a full plate at the ranch right now."

"I can do some of the work from here. Calves aren't due for another couple of weeks, so that gives me some time," she said. Zach could only give her advice. Amber was old enough to make her own decisions, and she would. He knew it, too, based on the look in his eyes.

"If that's the decision, I'd better track down this little one's parents," he finally said.

"What about a home paternity test? Don't they sell those at the drugstore?" Amber already had her cell phone out, checking out names of tests on the internet. "Do you think those are accurate?"

"Sometimes they are. Sometimes they aren't. This is too important to leave to chance," Zach stated.

"You're right about that." Rylan folded his arms.

"The courts will want me involved to prove paternity," Zach said. "They'll want me to control the chain of evidence. We'll get Dr. Logan out here to take the sample. Let me text Elise and tell her not to come. She probably won't want to get out in this weather anyway."

The fact that Rylan could be a father slammed into Amber. She couldn't see him waking up at three thirty in the morning for feedings or diaper changes until this moment. There was something about the look in his eye that said he would do whatever he needed to in order to care for his child.

Amber's chest squeezed at thinking about the baby's mother showing up and wanting to be a family. It was silly, really. Amber and Rylan had never dated. A relationship with her older brother's friend was completely out of the question, especially considering no one would clue her in as to why they'd stopped talking. And yet an inappropriate stab of jealousy struck anyway.

Did she want another baby? Was that the reason for the strange emotions coursing through her? The one she'd lost with her ex had nearly done her in emotionally. She couldn't even talk about the baby that had been stillborn, the divorce that had followed.

When she really thought about it…no. Amber had too many responsibilities at the ranch and in town.

Thinking about babies struck her as odd. She'd never been the type to sit around and daydream about weddings and kids. She'd never really been certain that having a family of her own was the right decision for her, especially after losing her parents, her baby, and then getting divorced before she turned twenty. She'd seen a few of her brothers find happiness and settle down. Marriage had been good for them.

Amber couldn't fathom trying again. Besides, she had too much to accomplish. And she may never decide to have a family of her own. It would take a special guy in her life to make her want those things again. He would have to be someone incredibly special to make her able to face another pregnancy.

And the funny thing was that she wasn't even ready to begin looking for him.

But, sitting in Rylan's kitchen, holding what could be *his* baby, she couldn't deny a certain pull toward the child.

Then again, those big brown eyes and round cheeks had a way of casting a spell on a person. *Quit being so cute, kiddo.*

Amber refocused on the conversation going on between Zach and Rylan. It involved a doctor and the court and words she never expected to hear in a conversation about Rylan. Fatherhood. Wow. It looked like he was about to grow up if this was real. Looking at his body—a body he'd filled out during his time in the military—it looked like Rylan had already accomplished that on his own.

Her heart stuttered when he caught her gaze. He also busted her staring at his chest. Her cheeks flamed. This was turning out to be a red-letter day.

He walked close to her as Zach made a phone call, presumably to Dr. Logan.

"Thank you for offering to stay, Amber." He started to say more, but she put her hand up to stop him.

"It's nothing." Her heart argued against her offer amounting to nothing. "Don't worry about it."

How long could it take to get answers?

Chapter Four

"I'm sure I would've heard gossip if Amber Kent had had a baby. So, who does this little bean belong to?" Dr. Logan smiled at Brooklyn. She cooed. Wow, Amber thought. Five kids definitely gave him the experience edge. Thankfully, he'd been on his way home from the hospital and didn't mind diverting for a few minutes to lend a hand.

Amber and her family had known Dr. Logan since forever. His green eyes were as warm as ever even though the rest of him was aging. He was graying everywhere else. He was a gentle man, fairly tall at five feet eleven inches but much shorter than Rylan. Dr. Logan kept himself in shape by running.

The times Amber headed into town in the morning she'd see him on a run. He was an honest man who'd been married to the same woman since graduating high school. They'd had five children, and the joke had always been that they needed one more to keep up with the Kents. Mrs. Logan and Amber's mother had been close friends. Amber's heart squeezed. Even though it had been years and she should be used to it by now, she still missed her mother. She missed her father, too, of course. But after losing her child, Amber could have used her mother to help get her through. The recent holidays left her feeling blue without her parents.

"She's not mine. We're trying to figure out if she belongs to Rylan Anderson," Amber said to the doctor with a wink. She'd asked to be the one to answer the door when he knocked.

"I'd heard he was back in town. Didn't realize he brought back a family." Dr. Logan wasn't being judgmental when he said it. He glanced past Amber. Seeing him made her miss her folks that much more, and between Brooklyn and her brothers' babies maternal feelings stirred inside Amber after shutting them off after losing her baby.

"Zach and Rylan are in the kitchen." She motioned toward the back of the house. She stopped short of walking in the next room. "Rylan had his world shaken up, Dr. Logan. He just learned about this little angel and has no idea if she's his."

"Oh. I see. Zach mentioned there was a question about the little girl. I didn't connect the dots. Forgive an old man." His smile lit up his eyes and made her think about her own pop. He would be close to the same age as Dr. Logan now. Her father's eyes had been hazel, like looking across the sea.

"Thanks for understanding." Amber's eyes started welling up. That was embarrassing. She shoved her feelings aside, wiped a rogue tear and focused on the baby in her arms.

Amber followed Dr. Logan into the kitchen. She'd believed that she'd dealt with her sense of loss with her parents a couple of years ago, but emotion brimmed just under the surface. "Thank you for coming, Dr. Logan," Zach said with an outstretched hand.

He took Zach's offering first and then Rylan's.

"How about you sit right here," Dr. Logan said to Amber, motioning toward the chair next to the kitchen table. "This won't take but a second."

He made goofy faces at Brooklyn. The baby laughed. He played peekaboo, and the little angel's laugh caused an ache in Amber's chest. Doc opened his medical bag and pulled out a swab. He used it to collect a sample from the inside of the little girl's cheek.

Rylan paced circles on the tile floor behind Amber. She avoided eye contact with her cousin because she could already read the disapproval on his features. He wouldn't want her around Rylan any more than her brother Will would.

Rylan had made a few mistakes, she'd give Will that much. And she knew deep down her brother still cared about his former best friend even though he'd refused to talk about him the first year Rylan was gone. Anyone who mentioned Rylan's name got a dirty stare before Will excused himself and left the room. Something had happened between them, and she couldn't for the life of her figure out what it had been. And she'd tried. She'd quietly asked around, but either no one knew or no one was talking. Knowing her brother, no one knew but Will and Rylan. Will had gone quiet and Rylan signed up for the military.

Will was stubborn. Especially when he thought he was right.

The problem was that she had no idea how her brother felt about Rylan anymore. Her relationships with her siblings had changed after losing their parents. In some ways the loss had brought them all closer. In others it had taken a toll. Everyone had been busy in the last few years changing their lives in order to take over their rightful places at the ranch.

Nothing felt settled. Of course, that could just be Amber. She was the broken one.

Brooklyn cooed once more at Dr. Logan, who could win Dad of the Year based on his exchange with the baby. In fact, Amber figured she could learn a few things from the man.

Again, the thought of Rylan being a dad struck a strange chord. She needed to get a grip. They were old friends and nothing more. He needed help and had been back in town only a week or two. He'd reached out to her as a friend, and she was helping because of their past and because the recent holiday season had her feeling melancholy. That was all. Her body might have an inappropriate reaction to seeing Rylan again, but logically she knew better than to put too much stock into it.

So the military had filled him out and he looked even more gorgeous than before, if that was even possible. That wasn't all. Something was different. They were both eight years older; both had changed.

"One more sample and I'll be on my way," Dr. Logan said, looking toward Rylan.

Amber figured that Rylan would want to know immediately about the results and part of her wanted to know, too. Again, the thought of Rylan being a dad blew her away. He hardly seemed old enough, but he very much was. Several of her brothers were married and had children.

Reality was a hard smack. When had everyone gotten this old?

Okay, granted, being in their twenties and early thirties wasn't exactly *old*. She meant when had everyone matured enough to have families of their own? It felt like only a minute had passed since she'd been running in the fields with one or more of her brothers and some of their neighbors playing Keep Away or Freeze Tag.

And now?

She'd blinked and everything was different.

"Any chance you can share the results with Rylan the minute they come in?" she asked the doctor.

"I think that would be okay as long as the sheriff doesn't have a problem with it," Dr. Logan answered.

All eyes flew to Zach.

"I'm fine with it." The sheriff raked his fingers through his hair. "I'd want to know as soon as possible if this was me. Official word is for the courts."

"Thank you," Amber said, and she could see some measure of relief on Rylan's face. Otherwise, he looked pretty out of his element.

The doctor finished his tests in a matter of minutes. He handed one to Zach and placed one in his carrying case. "I won't have the results until Monday. The lab's closed for the day."

Amber figured it was going to be an uncomfortable night, but they could power through.

"Thank you." Rylan walked Dr. Logan to the front door.

Amber turned to Zach. "There's a diaper bag with a handwritten note in it."

"I'll take it into evidence." Zach excused himself and then returned a minute later with a paper bag.

"It's in there," she said.

Zach was careful to remove the note. "Maybe we'll get lucky with a fingerprint match."

"Mine will be on there. Sorry." Amber wasn't sure

she wanted Brooklyn's mother to be in the criminal database. That would mean her mother had committed other crimes, which was not exactly ideal.

Amber's stomach performed that annoying flip-flop routine when Rylan came back into the kitchen.

"I better run. Let me know if Dr. Logan sends word to you, okay?" Zach held tight to the evidence bag that now had a companion.

"We will," Amber answered before Zach let himself out.

Rylan motioned toward the coffee machine on the counter. "You want another cup?"

"Yes, please." Amber didn't want to think about how right it felt to be in this man's kitchen. There was a lot she didn't know about Rylan, like what he'd been doing for the past eight years. "What did you do in the military?"

He rolled massive shoulders. "Not much. I was a diver."

She'd known a Navy SEAL once who used that line. It also meant that he wouldn't tell her much more. She glanced around the room. "You're still getting settled in?"

"Yep." He turned the tables on her when he asked, "What have you been up to for the past eight years?"

"I'm the one asking questions," she shot back.

"Why is that?" He picked up her coffee mug and walked toward the machine.

"You're the one who asked for my help, remember?" She wasn't ready to talk about her past with anyone.

"Is that how this works?"

"It is if you want me to stick around," she said playfully.

"I do. So, I guess you're in charge." He poured a cup and started the second.

"Be honest. How come you and my brother stopped talking?"

Rylan froze for a split second but then recovered quickly and went back to work. "People change."

"What's that supposed to mean?" Amber didn't see how two best friends could become so distanced in two seconds flat. She understood people growing apart or moving in different directions in life, but this had been like stepping in front of a bus.

"It's not important," he said, dismissing the conversation. He turned around with two mugs in his hands. "But she is, and that's my first priority right now." He motioned toward the baby.

He set the mugs down.

Amber bounced the little girl, who cooed. It was satisfying to be able to help with Brooklyn. Maybe Amber wasn't all thumbs at taking care of little ones after all. She was getting enough experience with her brothers recently, that was for sure.

"There's a cold front coming tonight," Rylan said.

"That does tend to happen this time of year." Christmas was a few weeks ago. It had always been Amber's favorite holiday. Except for the past few years. Since losing her parents, she hadn't found her footing. Being with her brothers and their families had been the best part about it. Amber couldn't help but notice the absence of her parents even more this time of year.

"All I have is what's in that diaper bag." He took a sip of coffee. "She'll freeze in what she's wearing."

"Don't be dramatic, Rylan. She'll be fine. You'll wrap her in extra blankets," she said.

"And what if she kicks them off? I'm a whirlwind sleeper. What if she's the same?" His look of concern was endearing. Her stomach performed another somersault routine. "Let's worry about getting some lunch first. Then we can think about sleeping arrangements later."

Rylan didn't speak for a few minutes. He looked tired and concerned.

"However this turns out will be okay, Rylan. You know that, right?" she asked.

"No, it won't."

RYLAN DIDN'T HAVE the first idea how to be a dad. He was probably going to damage the child beyond repair *if* she turned out to be his. Part of him was still holding out hope that there'd been some mistake. It wasn't Brooklyn's fault. The kid was adorable. He was the problem.

Besides, a mother would have to be desperate to leave her child with someone she hadn't seen in a year who'd never met the child. To make matters worse, he didn't even remember the child's mother. What kind of jerk did that make him?

"Tell me what you're thinking, Rylan." Amber's voice—a voice he'd thought about more than he should admit while he was overseas—cut through his heavy thoughts. Telling his best friend that he'd kissed his little sister before shipping off had been a disaster, especially after the mistakes Rylan had made. He didn't blame Will for not trusting him. Rylan hadn't deserved his friend's confidence.

Even so, Will's reaction had set Rylan off. Will had blown up. Rylan had gotten offended. He'd been so hotheaded back then. Ready to fight the world and, stupidly, his best friend when his reaction wasn't what Rylan was hoping for.

There was more to it than that. Rylan had been pushing boundaries and heading toward dangerous territory. Will had tried to intervene and talk him down from doing stupid things. What had Rylan's response been to his friend's concern? He'd told him to get a life and had gone off and messed up royally.

"I'm thinking that I'm in a whole mess of trouble." The baby was one thing. Rylan had come back to make amends for his mistakes. Now, his life had just gotten a whole lot more complicated.

"Well, it's no use feeling sorry for yourself," Amber said a bit more emphatically than he liked.

He couldn't help but smile. "That's not what I was doing."

"What do you call it then?" There was a hint of mischief in her eyes, and he didn't want to think it was sexy even though he did.

He missed talking to Amber. With her, conversation wasn't work like with most people. She had a quick wit and sharp sense of humor, but it was her intelligence that drew him in. Seeing her again was supposed to stop him from thinking about her. That, like many of his plans of late, had gone to hell in a handbasket the second he put eyes on the woman.

She was still beautiful. More so now that she had a few curves. She had big eyes, not saucers because that description would be way too plain. And they were the most beautiful shade of brown. Her nutmeg-colored hair fell past her shoulders in that braid. She'd grown it out a little more, and it looked good on her.

"Where do you think her mother could be?" Amber asked. She must've noticed that he'd been staring at her with the way her cheeks flushed.

"That's a great question," he said.

"A woman would have to be awfully desperate to convince a person to drop off an angel like this at a man's house sight unseen." Amber's brow shot up. "Why'd you really come back to Jacobstown?"

Rylan shrugged. He wasn't ready to talk about the real reasons, and there were many. He settled on, "It's where I'm from."

"I figured you'd end up in the city," she admitted.

"Fort Worth? Nah."

"No, I was thinking someplace farther than Fort Worth. Austin, maybe. San Antonio. I didn't think you'd come back here," she said.

"Austin's nice. I have work here, though," he said. What he meant to say was that he had work to do. He had retribution to pay, and would never be able to get on with life as a man if he didn't right a wrong. He didn't want to go into the details until he figured out how to go about it.

There was another reason why he'd come back to Jacobstown. He had nowhere else to go.

"You came back for a job?" she asked.

"Something like that," he said. "Why all the questions? Don't you think I should be here?"

"I never said that," she said quickly. "I'm just surprised. I figured you put this town behind you and didn't want to look back."

"I served in the military. I didn't sign up to live on Mars." A big part of him didn't want to look back at Jacobstown; facing this town again was harder than he expected. But he could never move forward until he made amends for the past. The Willow family deserved that and more.

"Why not?" she asked with a smirk.

"Mars doesn't have a Jacobstown," he quipped.

"You always said you couldn't wait to leave this town, to get out and make your mark on the world." She took a sip of coffee, which wasn't an easy feat with a baby in her lap. She managed to balance both without letting Brooklyn grab the cup.

"I was fifteen years old the last time I said that. What did I know?" He stood and walked over to the window. The wind had picked up, and he could see the oak tree in his backyard sway.

"Your head was filled with ideas about what you were going to do when you turned eighteen," she continued. She fell quiet for a few minutes, bouncing and playing with the baby on her lap. "Did you find what you were looking for out there?"

Rylan didn't answer.

Instead, he took another sip of coffee and contemplated the storm.

"It's going to get a lot worse out there. You okay with being here if it really comes down?"

Amber looked up at him and locked on to his gaze.

"A storm never stopped me, Rylan."

Chapter Five

"It's important to get the exact brand of formula or she can get an upset stomach. Think you can find everything on the list all right by yourself?" Amber asked Rylan after giving him a few items to purchase from the store for an overnight with the baby.

"Yes." The one word answer gave more of a hint that he was so far out of his element he didn't know where to begin.

Amber couldn't help but smile. Her heart pounded her ribs as she thought about spending the night alone with the former SEAL. She could admit to having had a childhood crush on her older brother's former best friend. Speaking of which, she still had a lot of questions about what had happened between the two of them. Based on the earlier conversation with Rylan, she wasn't going to get easy answers.

"What's so funny?" He stood at the front door, searching his pockets for his keys.

"Not a thing." Amber shouldn't break what little

confidence he seemed to have when it came to the baby. "But when was the last time you went shopping?"

"Yesterday," he shot back.

"Your keys are on the kitchen table, by the way." She couldn't help herself from smiling again.

Frustration came off Rylan in waves. He made eye contact, which did a whole bunch of things to Amber's stomach. Unwelcome things at that.

"Thanks." He stalked into the next room, and she heard his keys jingle a moment later. "You sure you'll be okay alone with her?"

"Yes." The fact that he was worried about the little bean caused Amber's heart to squeeze. There was something incredibly sexy about a strong and outwardly tough man's vulnerability when it came to protecting a baby.

Amber reminded herself that Brooklyn had a mother out there who could walk through that door any second. The woman had obviously tracked Rylan down. She held the cards until the paternity test came back. Again, the thought of Rylan being a dad hit hard.

"Where's the list I gave you?" she asked an uncharacteristically frazzled-looking Rylan.

He glanced around and checked his pockets again. This time, he came up with a crumpled piece of paper.

"I should come with you," she said.

"No child seat in my Jeep. Remember?" For a split second she saw the relief in his eyes. It shouldn't amuse her.

"Fine. I'll take her for a walk instead. She could use some fresh air." Amber stood.

"You sure it's not too cold outside?" His concern was evident in his wrinkled brow.

"Get out of here, Rylan. We'll be fine. I'll wrap her in a blanket if I have to." She shooed him out the door and followed him onto the porch. "Call if you get stuck on something, you hear? I'll have my phone with me at all times."

He nodded and then hopped off the porch.

Amber glanced around at the land, land that was as much part of her soul as the ranch her family owned. Texas was everything to her.

Rylan stopped before climbing inside his Jeep. He looked like he wanted to say something. It took a few seconds as he seemed to be searching for the words. "I owe you one for this big time, Amber."

"Go on, Rylan," she urged. Figuring out a way to keep an emotional distance was difficult when he stood there staring at her. Her stomach decided to flip like a gymnast again, and she took a deep breath in order to calm it down. She needed to collect her thoughts and keep control of her mental game.

He smiled one of those devastating Rylan smiles before backing out of the drive.

There was a serious chill in the air. Amber decided on that blanket. She walked inside and moved into the master bedroom, ignoring the sensual shivers racing across her skin at being in Rylan's personal space.

"Where's a blanket that won't swallow you whole?" she said to the baby.

Brooklyn smiled up at Amber.

"You sure are a cutie," Amber soothed, pleased that the little girl seemed to be happy. Amber was good with her nieces and nephews, but she'd had practice with them. This baby was little, and she couldn't hold this bean without thinking of her nieces and nephews as well as the one she'd lost.

More of those adorable dimples showed. Amber wiped a rogue tear and refocused. She couldn't go there mentally with the one she'd lost. It still hurt too damn much even though it had happened years ago.

The only blanket Amber could find was on the bed. She didn't want to wrap Brooklyn in the one he used for sleep. She moved to the bathroom and opened the cupboard, looking for a good-size, thick towel. She noted the size of the bathroom was perfect for one person.

In fact, the two-bedroom house was made for a single person. The space was in disarray, which was not Rylan's fault, but it was no place for an infant. There were unpacked boxes in the bedroom, too. It looked like one of the walls had been marked for demolition. Old wallpaper hung from walls in the bathroom and bedroom. This place was a construction nightmare. Also, the carpet seemed as old as the house. It had probably been a nice color of beige at one point. Now it was stained and had ripples so big from wear a person could trip over them. There was no way a baby could safely crawl around on this germy floor.

"How long did he say he'd lived here?" Amber said to Brooklyn because the little one seemed to like the sound of Amber's voice.

She located a towel in the hall cupboard, held it to her nose and sniffed it.

"Clean," she announced to the baby. "Are you ready to go outside for a walk?"

Brooklyn stuffed her fist in her mouth. Drool dripped from her chin.

"Are you an early teether?" Amber hadn't seen any teeth so far, but that didn't mean one wasn't trying to peek out of her gums. Three months old was early to be getting her first tooth, but it wasn't unheard of. Six months was the general rule of thumb, but with her nieces and nephews Amber had learned that while there were general guidelines, when it came down to it every child was unique.

Without her nieces and nephews, Amber would be lost right now. She'd never been the babysitting type until her oldest brother Mitch and his wife, Andrea, had had twins. Rea and Aaron were the first Kent babies and kicked off a baby boom at the ranch that Amber wanted no part of personally. She loved every bit of being an aunt. But babies of her own after what had happened? Amber didn't see herself going down that path again.

Besides, she'd always been the outdoorsy type and loved working long hours on the ranch. A fact she blamed on having five brothers. She was also the youngest, which probably should've made her spoiled rotten, but she had too much of her father's hard-working attitude for that nonsense. She'd never been one for inside chores. The only kind of cooking she was good at was for holidays or daily survival. The only remotely motherly thing she ever did was cook at Christmas, and that was because her mother had insisted. Lydia Kent had been revolutionary for her generation. She hadn't seen cooking as women's work, and Amber couldn't agree more. Mother had made a point of having all of her children pitch in for holiday meals. Everyone had grumbled about it growing up. And now, Amber couldn't be more grateful.

Because of her mother's ideals and stubbornness in the face of opposition, Amber and her brothers had been continuing the tradition of Crown Pork Roast with Cranberry Pecan Stuffing as a main course along with Make-Ahead Yeast Rolls and desserts like Apple-Bourbon Pie and Orange Bundt Cake.

They baked molasses crunch cookies, staying up too late in the week leading up to Christmas after daily chores were done.

The smiles on everyone's faces once they quit grumbling about helping and started rolling up their sleeves and working easily made up for the lost sleep. Their mother would turn up the radio that was locked on to the station that played nonstop Christmas carols. She practically danced around the kitchen. She used to joke that Dad got the children most of the year after the age of five but Christmas belonged to her.

She'd blocked out holiday memories in the years after losing her mother. Her father, a devoted husband, had joined his wife a few short years after her death.

Amber's mother was the bright light, the warmth, that everyone had migrated toward.

Brooklyn stirred in Amber's arms, and she ignored the pang in her chest as she stared at the little girl happily sucking on her fist. Amber put on her coat and then wrapped the baby in the towel like a burrito. She gathered Brooklyn in her arms and headed outside for some fresh air, reminding herself that she always got a little melancholy after the holidays.

Rylan lived in town in a neighborhood with quarter- to half-acre lots. It was nice to walk around the area. Make no mistake, she loved living on the ranch but this was pleasant, too. It seemed like a change of pace, and she could see how a kid might enjoy having neighbors close by. Amber had grown up with brothers and around ranch hands. Her only respite was her cousin Amy, who was also Amber's best friend.

Speaking of which, she owed Amy a phone call. She had been the one to warn Amber that Rylan had come back to Jacobstown. Amber had been caught off guard that her cousin had felt the need to approach the subject with caution. When Amber had cornered Amy about it, she'd acted like it was no big deal. But her cousin always had a reason for her actions. She was probably warning of the fireworks to come between Rylan and Will.

She'd traveled two blocks from Rylan's house before she snapped out of her mental walk down memory lane. There was a school playground at the end of the street, so she picked up the pace.

"You'll probably like going to the playground, right?" Amber was keenly aware that she was enjoying a conversation with a little one who had no ability to talk back. She was trying to distract herself from thinking about Rylan too much. He was never far from her thoughts.

The playground could use some updating, Amber thought as she climbed the four metal stairs to the smallest slide. She held on to a rail as she positioned herself at the top and then slid down. Brooklyn laughed. The park consisted of a slide, three swings and a seesaw. The wood chips needed replacing, she thought as she made her way to the swings. She made a mental note to tour other parks and see if she could form a neighborhood beautification committee. Everyone in the community would benefit from updated playground equipment, and there'd been great strides making the features safer in the last five years. A committee could evaluate parks across Jacobstown, identify the ones in the most need of new equipment and start from there.

Amber also needed to call home and let everyone know she wouldn't be back tonight. She had a load of hay in the bed of her truck that needed to be taken home at some point. Their bulk order was delayed and this would be enough to get them by until it's delivered.

"You like the swing, don't you?" Amber asked, pleased with herself for being able to make the little girl happy. Besides, she needed to keep her mind busy because her thoughts kept wandering to Rylan, and that was as productive as milking a boar. Get close enough to one of those and she'd end up hurt, too.

She half expected to hear from Rylan at some point. That he hadn't called so far was probably good news, but also worried her. Was he *that* lost? Or *that* embarrassed to ask for help? Her brothers wouldn't stop for help unless the car was on fire.

"You ready to go again?" she asked Brooklyn, and Amber's heart melted a little more when the little girl with the big eyes smiled up at her.

If the slide was popular, the swing was like Christmas morning to Brooklyn. Amber held on to the little angel while swinging so long her arms felt like they might fall off.

"Okay, little miss. We better head home." She figured the baby would be hungry soon.

It was chilly outside so they'd had the entire park to themselves, which was good given the size. There were enough houses nearby to warrant further digging into an expansion.

Amber held Brooklyn to her chest and marveled at the warmth from the little bundle. As she turned the corner toward Rylan's house, the hairs on the back of her neck pricked. She had a strange feeling that someone was watching her, but it was probably just her imagination. Her nerves were on edge.

Amber glanced behind her and quickened her pace. She heard a car in the distance. It was otherwise a quiet Saturday afternoon. She surveyed the sidewalk across the street, looking for movement. There were tall pines and mesquite trees lining the street. It was windy, and the temperature felt like it was dropping with every forward step she took.

Something or someone moved down the street. The person was too far away to get a good look. Amber quickened her stride, needing to get to Rylan's house as soon as possible. It felt like fire ants crept across her skin. She'd feel more comfortable behind a locked door at this point. Unfortunately, that meant moving toward the person—and she was certain the object was a him now—who'd ducked behind a tree.

Amber hugged Brooklyn tighter to her chest. The baby didn't seem to mind. She happily cooed and blew raspberries on her fist, unaware of the possible danger.

Another twenty feet and Amber would have the baby inside.

This probably wasn't the time to think about the fact that she'd left Rylan's door unlocked. Of course, she didn't have a key.

The figure moved. It was tall and broad, so her initial guess was right. He had to be male.

Brooklyn stirred and let out a sad little cry. Amber's heart battered her ribs as she soothed the baby. She hoped that Zach could get a hit from the description Rylan gave of the man who'd dropped Brooklyn off and ran.

Who did that? Granted, people could be desperate for money. She'd been blessed to grow up in a house where she never wanted for anything. But this was a life, a child. Who could be so cold as to drop a baby and run?

Amber couldn't get inside the house fast enough. She'd lost visual contact with the male, and her nerves were pulled taut. Rylan's house was close. So, Amber broke into a run. Brooklyn fussed louder as she was bounced up and down so Amber slowed her pace to a fast walk.

"It's okay," Amber soothed.

She cut across the front lawn, praying the man was gone. She wasn't exactly fast with a baby in her arms, and Brooklyn was most likely picking up on Amber's stress. She'd read somewhere that babies could do that. They could absorb emotions and react. She willed herself to be calm and soothing.

It was too early to be relieved, but making it onto the porch felt like a win. Noise from behind startled her. She spun around to investigate.

Her back thudded against the door when she saw him. He was too close. There was no way she could get inside before he got to her.

The tall male wore a hoodie, scarf and jeans. Sunglasses shielded his eyes. Amber couldn't make out the details of his face.

"Fire," she screamed at the top of her lungs. She'd been taught by her law enforcement cousin never to yell for help in a situation such as this. He'd taught her that people reacted to hearing the news of a fire.

It might be self-preservation instinct and them wanting to make sure their property wasn't about to burn, but she didn't care.

Brooklyn went into full-on crying mode, and Amber could only pray someone heard her own screams over the sound of the baby.

The male sneered at her as he closed the gap between them, his mouth and nose were the only things visible. As he neared, she smelled tobacco and figured the scent would be burned into her nostrils for the rest of her life.

"Fire," she shouted again, but feared the neighbors were too far away to hear. It was cold enough for windows and doors to be closed, and the wind howled. She had to think of something. She had to assume the man was there to take Brooklyn, and no way was she letting him walk away with the innocent child without a fight.

Running would do no good. Amber wouldn't get far while holding a baby. Besides, this guy had to have run behind the houses in order to sneak up on her like that, and he didn't seem winded. He was tall, maybe six feet, with a runner's build.

When the male was close enough to reach for the baby, Amber started memorizing details of what little she could see of his face. His skin was light, pale. His eyebrows red. He had a small mole on the left side of his nose.

"I don't have anything for you," she shouted with more authority than she owned. "Step away."

His gloved hands were reaching for the baby. No doubt he'd be stronger than her. Amber had seconds to make her move.

She let him get close, so close she could smell his awful breath. In one quick motion, she stepped into him and brought her right knee up hard into his groin. She ducked out of his grasp as he winced and coughed.

She'd barely bought a few seconds. Making a run for her truck was her best option. She'd left the keys under the mat on the driver's side and maybe could make it inside without him catching up by some miracle. Driving with a baby in her arms was not ideal.

Brooklyn was screaming at the top of her lungs as Amber hopped off the porch. She made it all of two steps when his hands gripped her arms. She struggled against his grasp, but it was like being locked in a viselike grip.

All she could think to do was to drop down, but he stopped her. He was strong. Too strong. Brooklyn was fussing and fidgeting. It was all Amber could do to hang on to the little girl.

In the next second, Amber was being spun around and the baby pulled from her arms. She couldn't let this happen. She couldn't let this man get away with Brooklyn. And she couldn't stop him, either.

He ripped the crying baby from her arms.

It dawned on Amber that he would have the same problem she did. Trying to run with a baby was next to impossible. So, Amber grabbed onto his neck. She didn't want to risk hurting the baby, but if she let this criminal take off with Brooklyn, the child's life could be over before it got started. What kind of a person tried to steal a baby?

Amber fisted his metal frame sunglasses as she was dragged forward a few steps. She crushed them against his face.

He ground out a few curses before giving a shake that was so hard she lost her grip. She kept repeating the word *fire* at the top of her lungs, praying someone would hear her.

Amber clawed at his right arm until she was able to get in front of him. She grabbed Brooklyn and before he could rip the baby out of her arms again, she heard the sounds of an approaching vehicle coming. She risked a glance and saw a Jeep.

The assailant must've seen it, too, because he sprinted in the opposite direction.

Amber held Brooklyn to her chest as she checked the little girl for any signs of being hurt. Tears streamed down Amber's face at the thought of what had just happened, what *could've* happened.

The Jeep came roaring up and came to an abrupt stop. In the next second, Rylan was out the driver's door and giving chase to the attacker, who'd disappeared behind the neighbor's house.

Amber wasted no time locating the keys. She wouldn't give that jerk an escape route if he doubled back.

Heart pounding, she darted toward the house and locked them both inside.

Hands shaking, she managed to calm the baby by rocking her.

Stomach lurching, she conceded to being rattled as she sat down and balanced the baby in her lap so she could call Zach.

Chapter Six

Rylan lost track of the hooded male two blocks east of the park down the street from his house. The guy was a good sprinter, and Rylan figured that he had a vehicle tucked away over there on the ready. He must've planned for the run scenario, which meant there was premeditation on his part. Any thought this could have been a spur of the moment decision, however minuscule, died.

Frustration was a gut punch. The only reason the jerk got away in the first place was because Rylan had hesitated at the get-go, wondering if he should stick with Amber and the baby in order to protect them.

The decision to run was predicated on two things. Trying to find out who that little girl was and who she belonged to. Both of those might still be a mystery, but someone seemed determined to take her from Amber.

Blood ran hot in Rylan's veins. The kid didn't need to belong to Rylan for him to want to make sure she wasn't put in harm's way.

Was this the reason the girl's mother had found him? More questions surfaced as he broke into a run back to his place. Was he even the father? Or had a desperate woman sought him out for his ability to keep her baby safe? Had this been the move of a woman who had no choices left?

Rylan of all people couldn't judge another person for those actions. He'd been in his fair share of circumstances that had caused him to act out of character. Hell, he'd taken and run with a lie and tangled his best friend in it, too. That had cost him—he'd lost someone who he'd considered to be the brother he'd never had. Will Kent wasn't a liar, but he'd lied to keep Rylan out of jail. Rylan had been young and stupid. He'd made too many mistakes thinking he wasn't worth anything. Not even his best friend could convince him otherwise.

Rylan had a stubborn streak a mile long. And just to prove his friend wrong, Rylan started drinking and hanging around with the wrong crowd in nearby Collinsville. He'd done things to be ashamed of. Yeah, he could play the abandoned kid card all day long. Down deep, he'd known better. The military had helped him get his anger out. He'd gone in looking for a fight and found one. He'd hoped that he'd come out a better man for it.

If that baby turned out to be his child, he wouldn't shy away from the responsibility. He did need to find the kid's mother and learn what the drop-and-run routine had been all about.

"Rylan, what happened? I was scared half to death. Get in here." Amber's eyes were wide as she stood in the open doorway, the baby fussing in her arms.

"I lost him." He stepped inside, chest heaving, allowing her to usher him in.

"At least he didn't get her." Amber closed and locked the door behind him. "Zach's on his way. I called him immediately. He should be here any minute."

For the moment Rylan needed to catch his breath.

"He was wearing sunglasses, and I couldn't get a good look at his eyes. He wore a hoodie and scarf, too. His skin was pale, and his eyebrows were red. And he had a small mole on the left side of his nose." Stress lines creased her forehead. "I smashed his sunglasses into his face to stop him from running away. Maybe there's a piece out there. It might give Zach some DNA to work with. I'm pretty sure I scratched his face up, so he'd be easily identifiable if he showed up in public. Plus, there should be some of his DNA under my fingernails."

"That was smart thinking, Amber." He should have known she'd be savvy enough to leave a trail for Zach. Facial marks would be difficult to hide in a public place. If this person was part of the Jacobstown community, he wouldn't be able to walk around freely until his face healed. All law enforcement would be on the lookout.

"What about prints? It looked like you two were struggling for the baby," he said.

"Zach won't have any luck there. The guy wore gloves." She shook her head for emphasis.

"You know what?" Rylan paced. Nothing inside him wanted to say these next words. "After you give Zach your statement, I want you to go home. Brooklyn and I will make it through the night okay. We'll figure it out."

The thought of being alone with a baby for an entire night sent an icy chill up his back. He had no knowledge of babies and no particular skills with them, either. Hell, he hadn't been around any until this little one.

"Absolutely not, Rylan."

"Look. I have more supplies in the Jeep. I'll get those and take over with her." He could be stubborn when he needed to be, and this situation called for it. Putting Amber in danger was never meant to be part of this deal. Now that he realized his mistake he needed to fix it ASAP.

"Don't go out there yet," she warned. "And I'm not leaving you alone with her. Do you even know how to change her diaper?"

"How hard can it be?" he asked.

She harrumphed and her jaw set, like when she was determined about something.

"Don't go digging your heels in the sand, Amber," he warned. "When I called for help earlier, I had no idea what I was committing you to. If anything happened to you it would be my…"

The look of understanding that overtook her features stopped him dead in his tracks.

"You called me because you knew I could help. How could you have known there'd be an attempted kidnapping?" She stared at him. "I'm not leaving you stranded when you need a friend, Rylan. I'm not built that way, so it won't do any good to argue. Besides, she's taken to me and I won't abandon her until we know who this angel's mother is and why she saw fit to drop her on your doorstep. Now that that's settled—"

A knock at the door interrupted her speech.

"That's probably Zach. I got this." Rylan knew Amber well enough to know when he'd lost an argument. It might've been years, but that same stubborn streak he'd noticed when they were teens seemed to have grown.

Zach stood on the porch. Rylan opened the door and invited him inside.

"Is the baby okay?" Zach asked before crossing the threshold.

"Yes."

"And how about Amber?" Zach didn't miss a beat.

"She is."

"Make sure she stays that way." Zach's tone issued a warning.

"Hold on there, Zach." Rylan put his hand on the sheriff's shoulder. "I just spent the past five minutes trying to convince her to leave. If you think I brought her into this knowing it could turn into a cluster—"

"Don't put words in my mouth, Rylan." The welcome home tone was gone from Zach's voice now. The man's words had hit hard.

"I didn't." Rylan heard the defensiveness in his own tone—defensiveness because the conversation he needed to have with her brother Will was on Rylan's mind.

AMBER DESCRIBED THE ATTACKER the best she could as she recounted her story to Zach. Her cousin nodded and scribbled down a few notes while she spoke. She could almost see his wheels turning, and he did a heck of a job not freaking out that she'd been part of the attack.

Rylan had already warned her about sticking around. After spending a little time with Brooklyn, Amber was hooked. She couldn't step aside while that little girl's future was so uncertain. Besides, Kents weren't made to walk away from danger. Kents stuck together and Kents stuck around. Her brothers and cousin hated to admit it during times like these, but she was no different from them. Not one would turn a blind eye to someone in need or in danger. Granted, she was the baby of the family and that fact had her siblings trying to play protector from time to time. Lucky for her, she'd grown up with five brothers to ensure she could handle herself in almost any situation.

Case in point, the attempted abduction had been stressful and her nerves were still shaky, but she'd managed to ward off the attack. Brooklyn was safe because Amber had been there.

"I broke his sunglasses, and I'm hoping something is left of them in the front yard." Before she could finish, Zach was on his way to the door. His back was turned so she couldn't see the look of panic she knew would be there at the admission.

The baby had had a bottle, which seemed to be enough to keep her satisfied. She was back to sucking on her fist. So, Amber hopped up, settled Brooklyn in her arms and followed.

The sun was starting its descent. This time of year, that meant it was a little after five o'clock. The yard was visible as they searched.

"This is where it happened." She pointed to the spot, and thinking about what had happened gave her a chill. So much could've gone wrong. Brooklyn could be in the hands of that man, who couldn't want her for good reasons. An honest man with good intentions would've knocked on the door and explained the situation calmly. Only someone with something to hide would try to rip a child out of a stranger's arms.

She knew to stay back and let Zach do his job. Trampling all over his crime scene wouldn't help. Rylan seemed to realize it, too. He stayed with her, and she could see the anger on his face. She figured the anger was for what had almost happened to Brooklyn even though a little piece of her wanted the anger to be for her, too.

It was a silly notion and one best left alone.

Amber tucked that idea away with all the other up-to-no-good thoughts racing in her head whenever he was near. He'd always had that effect on her. Well, not always. She'd thought him to be pretty darn annoying in middle school. High school had turned around her feelings toward him. But then his mother had died and he'd gone inside himself. He shut out all his old friends, and rumor had it that he'd gotten involved with a bad crowd in Collinsville.

She'd kept busy with the ranch and with school over the years. And then her mother had gotten sick. She and her brothers became orphans when her dad died a few years later. Granted, they'd been adults when that had happened. But none of them had truly ever gotten over losing their parents. Did anyone ever?

Coming from a tight-knit family had made them feel the losses that much more. And then everyone had scattered like buckshot in order to handle family business. She'd always known their family had each other's backs; that was a given. But no one ever talked about losing their parents or how that had changed everything. How that had changed the family's dynamic.

"Got something." Zach put on a pair of rubber gloves and retrieved a paper bag from his SUV. He returned to the spot he'd zeroed in on, careful as he stepped so as not to trample on evidence, and then squatted. Metal glinted in the sunlight as he picked up what looked like a piece of sunglass frame. He held it up toward the sun like he was examining a prize. "Between this and the DNA under your fingernails, we might have the break we need."

Amber had been around law enforcement long enough to realize this was too early to expect good news and that the evidence would have to be sent to a crime lab. Getting results could take weeks if not months depending on how busy the lab was.

After examining the area, Zach motioned for them to go inside. He was a few steps behind them because he put the evidence bag into his locked SUV for safekeeping.

Zach spun around on her the minute the door was

closed. His gaze flew to Rylan. "Do you mind giving us a minute to talk?"

Rylan locked gazes with Amber like he was checking to make sure that's what she wanted before he complied.

She nodded.

"I'll be in the kitchen if anyone needs me." Rylan winked and she smiled as he left the room.

"I don't like you being anywhere near this case." Zach cornered Amber. She sidestepped him and moved to the couch.

The minute she turned on him, ready to put up an argument, he brought his hand up to stop her.

"I do realize that I have no authority in which to make that request, and I also know that you aren't the type to be told what to do under any circumstances. But hear me out because I'm only saying this because I care about you."

"Fine. What do you want to say to me, Zach?"

His gaze moved from her to the baby and back. "She hasn't left your side since the last time I was here, has she?"

"Nope." Amber had no plans to abandon this little angel, either. She also had no plans to defend herself or try to convince him this was different.

Before she could respond, Zach blew out a sharp breath.

"I figured that would be the case." He sounded resigned to that end.

"So, what's next?" There was no use going down the road of him trying to talk her out of staying.

"I'm not finished," he said.

"Really? Because you know as well as I do that I'm not leaving this house until this girl is in safe hands. She's been through a lot already, and I don't want to traumatize her further by abandoning her." Those last words nearly caught in her throat. She coughed to clear them. "I know this situation stinks and none of us realized how dangerous it was going to be, but none of this is her fault. She's taken to me, and I have no plans to leave Rylan alone overnight with a child when he has no experience caring for one."

Brooklyn had leaned into Amber, and she was rubbing the little girl's back.

"What if that guy comes back? What if he brings others with him? We have no idea what we're dealing with here."

"All good points. I was thinking that maybe I could ask Rylan to stay over at the ranch tonight—"

"I'm not going where I'm not wanted." Rylan appeared in the doorway to the kitchen, and she'd known he was listening.

"I just invited you," she countered.

"You're not the problem." Rylan positioned his

feet in an athletic stance and folded muscled arms over his broad chest.

"Then who is?" she asked.

"That's between me and your brother. Trust me when I say that door is closed." Rylan's voice was steady, even. She wondered if it took much effort to come off that way. He and her brother had been close. It made no sense that they were still at odds.

"I can speak to my brother—"

"Like I already said, not an option. Can we just leave it at that?" Rylan's granite features gave away nothing, and he was a bull when he wanted to be. "You didn't leave when I told you to. I respect that. Now, you need to return the favor."

He made a good point. One she knew better than to argue.

"It might not be safe to stay here, Rylan. Have you considered that?" Those words seemed to sink in as he nodded.

"What are we dealing with here?" he asked Zach.

"The worst-case scenario is an illegal baby adoption ring. These groups are high stakes, and there's a lot on the line since they work outside the law. People who don't want their name in the press or who can't adopt a baby by legal means turn to folks like these." Zach wasn't trying to scare them. Amber knew that. He was putting his cards on the table. "There's generally a lot of money at stake, and that tends to draw very good criminals to the business."

"One of which I was able to stop because of the training you and my brothers gave me growing up," Amber pointed out.

"Once they know who and what they're dealing with, they'll come back more prepared next time." Zach's jaw set.

"They aren't the only ones," she started to say, but her cousin interrupted with a hand in the surrender position.

"Granted, what you did a little while ago might've saved the baby's life. Hell, I'm proud of you. The problem is that we don't know who she belongs to. We haven't established paternity, and technically have no rights to keep her." Zach's words hit harder than Amber had thought possible.

Being with Brooklyn was always going to be a temporary situation. So, why was Amber letting herself get so attached to the little bean?

She decided it was nothing more than protective instincts kicking in. Who wouldn't want to ensure this kid was okay? And maybe there was something motherly inside Amber after all. She'd doubted it after losing her own child within hours of his birth. Prior to getting pregnant, she'd never considered herself the marriage and kids type. But, hey, there was nothing wrong with being a fabulous aunt. Those were in short supply from what she'd heard.

And she loved the land, working on the ranch, being part of something bigger than just herself. She was helping build her family's legacy. How would she leave all that behind? She'd become a mom and then what? Scale back her work? Feel exhausted all the time? Not this pony.

"Something's off here. Doesn't this sort of thing usually happen with newborns?" Amber asked.

"I agree with the first part of what you said. But, no, this is a problem for the first year, to year and a half. Generally, kids older than that are safe from these kinds of people because couples want babies." Zach tucked his notebook inside his front shirt pocket and his eyes zeroed in on Amber. "If you insist on being here, I'll put extra security on the block just in case."

"Thank you, Zach." That should deter the jerk from making a return trip.

"Trust me when I say you don't want your brother finding out about this from someone other than the two of you," Zach said.

"Honestly, this situation might right itself by morning. We'll get Rylan's test results back and go from there." What were the chances he was the father anyway? They had to be slim, right? He couldn't remember being with anyone during the time in question.

And, besides, she'd make the call to Will.

Enough time had passed. Whatever had happened between her brother and Rylan would surely have blown over by now. How bad could it have been?

Chapter Seven

Zach was gone. The baby was fed, washed and asleep. Amber had washed her own face and borrowed a toothbrush in order to brush her teeth. Thankfully, Rylan had an unopened spare. They'd dined on leftover pizza earlier, and the day's events had left her beyond tired, considering days on the ranch started at four o'clock in the morning.

"Got any clothes I can change into?" she asked Rylan, who stood at the bathroom door holding Brooklyn.

It was probably just the day Brooklyn had had, but trying to put her down to sleep on a makeshift bed on the floor was totally out of the question. That little girl's eyes had shot open the second there was no more human contact. At least she hadn't been so disturbed that she couldn't go back to sleep right away the minute she'd been picked up and cuddled.

Rylan had Brooklyn, and Amber was almost amused at how uncomfortable he looked. This was the first break from holding Brooklyn that Amber had had since meeting the little bean. Her arms burned and literally felt like they might fall off. Amber also tried to ignore how right it felt to spend the day with Brooklyn.

She was a good baby. That was the extent to which Amber would allow herself to examine her feelings. And it was most likely the marriage and family boom at the ranch that had her comfortable with a child in the first place. If this had been a few years ago... Amber stopped right there. *This* never would've been a thing.

The family cattle business had never been so successful, and her innovation with organics had heralded the ranch into the future and was a large part of the reason for the success.

Of course, she could admit to feeling like she was missing out on something lately. But that *something* couldn't possibly be a baby. Amber had spent a long time convincing herself of that. Even so, being with Brooklyn fulfilled a need Amber didn't realize she had. It was probably just the growing Kent brood that had her questioning her stance on no longer wanting children of her own. Besides, she'd never survive that heartache again if something went wrong.

"I can take her back once I'm settled," she said as he stood there looking at the two of them.

An emotion passed behind Rylan's dark eyes that under different circumstances she'd recognize as desire. But that was probably just her mind playing tricks on her, seeing what it wanted to see. Rylan had never seen her as more than a little pain in the rear who'd followed him and Will around like a lost puppy. Okay, the lost puppy bit was probably being dramatic.

"Follow me," he finally said. She did and tried not to notice how cute his backside was. It was, no doubt about it, but that wasn't what she liked about Rylan.

Her high school crush had that mysterious troubled quality. He was a bad boy who was good deep down. Seriously hot. Wasn't that what every girl wanted? Finding a good bad boy was like owning a sweet horse that ran fast. Or meeting a unicorn.

Amber pushed those unproductive thoughts aside when she nearly bumped into said cute backside when Rylan abruptly stopped in front of her. It was probably her overwrought emotions that had her thinking about such silly things, like high school crushes.

First and foremost, she and Rylan had been friends. He'd been two years ahead of her in school.

And as long as she was admitting things to herself, she'd go ahead and say that he was a good guy. Sure, he'd started down a bad path but going into the military seemed to straighten him out.

A lesser man would've pushed this baby on the first person he could. He would've insisted Zach take her or allowed Child Protective Services to whisk the little girl away with a random family. No matter what Rylan said or thought of himself, he was a decent person.

"There are boxers in that drawer and T-shirts in the one below it." He motioned toward the dresser. She had to remind herself to breathe for seeing that baby sleeping so comfortably on his shoulder. A lightning bolt struck, like she needed to be more attracted to the man. What was it about a tough guy who could be so tender when handling something so vulnerable? A man like that was far more tempting than ice cream. And Amber liked ice cream.

Rylan walked to the door. He stopped at the threshold and hesitated for just a few seconds. Heat flushed through Amber, warming her in places she didn't want to think about with the baby in the room. With a sharp breath he left the room and closed the door behind him.

By the time Amber changed and walked into the living room, Rylan was studying his phone. He didn't look up, but he nodded toward the couch.

"You sure you don't want to sleep in the other room?" he asked.

"Definitely." She didn't want to sleep in sheets that had his masculine outdoorsy and campfire scent. She was no idiot. She wasn't doing that to herself on purpose. It was silly that she felt this strong of an attraction to Rylan after all these years. And embarrassing. Especially since he clearly still saw her as a friend. Even if he didn't, what would that mean? The two of them would never make it in the long run. They were about as opposite as two people could be. She loved the stability of the ranch and having family around, while staying in one place seemed to suffocate Rylan once he'd turned eighteen. As soon as he fixed up the Parker place, he'd get the itch to move on. Amber had no plans to get remarried. She'd shut that possibility off years ago when she'd married at eighteen, gotten pregnant almost immediately and lost both husband and child in less than six months. She'd begun her adult life as a divorcée, and that wasn't exactly a title she'd wanted to keep on her résumé.

She'd been young and infatuated. Amber had never been the type to sit around and dream about her wedding day. If she did get married again and, honestly, she couldn't see that as a possibility, then she'd go down to the courthouse and not make a big to-do over it.

Thinking back, her marriage had been the unhappiest time in her life. Before that, she'd felt free and full of possibilities. When she was little, her brothers used to tease her that she and Amy were like wild horses. Amber especially because she used to sneak into the barn and open the pens to let out the stock. Pop used to round them up and put them back in the stable. Amber would get in a whole mess of trouble, but she'd argue right back. When she was right, she was determined. When she thought she was right, she was unstoppable. She could hear her argument, her words to her father now. Wild horses had to be broken in order to be tamed. Not loved, broken. She couldn't think of a worse fate.

Being married had felt a lot like being shoved into a pen. Amber had accepted the proposal on impulse. The pregnancy came six weeks later, and she'd already realized being married wasn't for her. She'd kept quiet for the pregnancy's sake, figuring it was meant to be. That was the last time she second-guessed her instincts. They rarely failed her.

Amy and Isaac, from ranch security, had been on and off for the past couple of years. They were doing a terrible job of keeping their relationship a secret. Apparently, they were *on* again. What did it say about Amber that she was the Lone Ranger now?

There was a makeshift bed on the sofa. Rylan had pulled the back cushions off the couch and placed a rolled up blanket to soften the edge.

"You'll wear a hole in that carpet if you don't stop." Amber watched Rylan take another lap around the room.

"I was afraid if I stopped she'd wake up and cry again. I didn't want you up all night because of my rookie mistake," Rylan said.

"You want me to take her now?" Amber held out her arms because one look in his desperate eyes gave her the answer. "Looks like you've finally met your match, Rylan Anderson."

He gave her a resigned look.

"What do you need?" Relief brightened his stressed-out features when he handed over the baby successfully.

"Nothing I can think of. We'll be good." She lowered her voice to church-quiet as she balanced the baby and positioned herself in a somewhat comfortable position on the sofa. "Other than maybe the lights."

Rylan shut off all lights but one, a side table lamp with a soft glow.

"You going to sleep?" Amber bit back a yawn.

"Doubt if I can." He settled into a side chair.

"Deputy Perry is parked out front. Zach will most likely patrol the area all night. It's probably never been safer to grab some sleep. But if it would make you feel better, we could go in shifts." Her cousin wouldn't risk anything happening to her. He'd always been protective just like her brothers. Things had gotten even more tense with the crimes that had seemed to follow the Jacobstown Hacker and that first heifer discovery weeks ago.

"I'll wake you if I get tired, but I'm used to going days at a stretch." Of course, he would be. He'd only just gotten out of the military. She was pretty sure a mission wouldn't have him sleeping every night at the Ritz.

Silence stretched between them. The only sound Amber could hear was the baby's breathing. So many thoughts raced in Amber's mind. Technically, she didn't know Rylan any longer. He had no idea about her life, what she'd been through since the last time she'd seen him. And she had no idea who he really was anymore.

"Why'd you call me?" she asked out of the blue.

"You want the honest answer?"

"If it's a good one," she teased.

"I have no idea. You were the last friend I had in Jacobstown and the first one who came to mind," he said. "You've changed—"

"Well, so have you," she quickly countered, hearing the defensiveness in her own voice.

"Hold on. I meant that in a good way. You're older—"

She issued a grunt, stopping him cold.

"You're not a little kid anymore. You're a grown woman. Beautiful."

"Well, now you're doing a little better." She figured he'd added that last part to keep her from giving him a hard time. She'd accept the compliment anyway. "You ever think about becoming a daddy, Rylan?"

"No. I'm not anywhere near where I want to be in life, and I don't want to do that to a kid. But if the test proves she's mine, it doesn't matter what I think, does it?" The question was rhetorical. His tone left no room for doubt that he'd do the right thing by Brooklyn.

There was another long pause where neither spoke. After all these years, it should be awkward to be in a dark room alone with someone she knew from her childhood. But this was Rylan. She couldn't feel anything but at home with him. An annoying little voice warned her that she was alone with a stranger, but it wasn't difficult to quash.

"What are we going to do if he comes back?" she asked.

"This time, we'll be ready." That statement had so much finality to it Amber had no doubt that Rylan meant every word. He had the skills to back it up, too.

Amber shut the thought down. Because Rylan's protectiveness over the baby lying across her chest stirred Amber's heart in ways she couldn't allow or afford.

Conversation trailed off when Amber could no longer hold her eyes open. When she opened them again, she heard Rylan's steady breathing. His shirt was off, and in the dim light she could see his muscled chest.

An ache welled up from deep within.

RYLAN BLINKED HIS EYES open the second Amber shifted her weight.

"You're awake," she said, sounding caught off guard.

"I was never asleep. My eyes were resting." He rubbed the scruff on his chin and then raked a hand through his dark, thick hair.

"Said every man I've ever met who was actually sleeping." She laughed. Her laugh, hell, her voice, had a musical quality to it. This wasn't the time to get inside his head about why it was her laugh he'd heard when an enemy gunman stood over him with an AR-15 pointed at the center of his forehead. He'd told himself it was natural for childhood memories to come back when a man faced death. And she did have a great laugh.

"I've been thinking about where I might've been about twelve months ago. I was stationed in San Antonio last year and had a few weekends off. Several of us guys used to drive over to Austin. They did some partying." The disappointment on her face struck like a physical blow. "I haven't had a drink in six years, three hundred and twenty-four days. Except possibly that weekend."

"Oh." The one word and the way it was spoken conveyed pity. He didn't want that from Amber. "I'm sorry. I didn't realize that about your drinking. I knew it had gotten a little out of control before you left but—"

"My low point was good for me because it made me realize that I had a problem. I saw the man in the mirror one sober morning and knew that wasn't who I wanted to be. Not on weekends, not on leave, not anymore," he said. "Before that I did a few stupid and reckless things. None of which involved not using protection no matter who I was with or how much I'd had to drink."

The women he'd spent time with knew the deal. He was upfront about his mind-set. He'd always shied away from any woman who was interested in anything more than one night of mutually consensual and amazing sex.

"I'm sorry you went through all that," she said, and the sincerity in her voice made him realize just how alone he'd been all these years.

It was fine. His choice. But this was the first time his life seemed lonely when he thought about it. The possibility of fatherhood was probably what had him going inside himself, searching for redeeming qualities that might make him worthy of bringing up that little girl on his own. He had no plans to let her down.

Amber tried to sit up and the baby stirred.

"I need to use the restroom. Think you can handle her for a few minutes?" she asked.

He nodded, deciding not to point out the fact that he might be doing that for a heck of a lot longer than a few minutes. The idea should stress him out, and it did, but not as much as he expected. He'd had a few hours to let the possibility sink in.

There was no going back now. If the call that

came in said he was Brooklyn's father, so be it. He'd make sure that girl had a real childhood with dolls and dance classes even if he had to work two jobs to do it. Reality was a gut punch. Wasn't that what his mother had done? His father hadn't bothered to stick around long enough to get to know Rylan. That wasn't the life he wanted for Brooklyn. Staying in Jacobstown might not be an option. Work was sparse here. He'd have better luck and get more pay if he moved to Fort Worth or Dallas.

The thought of leaving Jacobstown hit harder than expected, but he could finish updating this house and then rent it out for income. He stopped himself right there. One step at a time. He didn't need to know how to finish the journey. He only needed to take the first steps. And that meant being okay with whatever news Dr. Logan delivered.

But first he needed to track down the baby's mother and find out what trouble she'd gotten herself into. Only a desperate mother would abandon her child.

Brooklyn squeezed her eyes shut before letting out a little cry. Panic set in. Was she hungry? Did she need a diaper change? Of course, she would need that. Didn't babies go to the bathroom almost constantly?

Thankfully, Amber returned before the baby could wind up a good cry. She brought a bottle back with her, and Brooklyn settled down almost immediately. She'd shown him how to feed the baby earlier, so he took her, figuring he needed the practice.

"You want me to burp her?" she asked him almost the second Brooklyn finished her bottle.

He nodded. There was an emotion behind Amber's eyes when she looked at the little girl that Rylan couldn't exactly pinpoint. Whatever it was ran deep.

"Will you teach me how to change her?" he asked as Amber passed the baby back to him. He did his level best not to sound as helpless as he felt when it came to taking care of the baby.

"It's easier than you think. Come on." The spark in Amber's eyes shouldn't stir his heart like it did. She could always make the most mundane thing seem like an adventure.

She dropped to the floor next to the diaper bag in the middle of the living room and waved him over. "Put her down on her back."

He was probably as awkward-looking as all hell, but he managed to set Brooklyn down gently without causing her to cry. The minute he withdrew his hands she kicked up a storm, and her sad face nearly broke him. "What did I do wrong?"

"Hold on there, little bean." Amber patted the little girl's tummy. Brooklyn wound up to cry, but Amber tickled her belly and Brooklyn laughed instead. The sound of her voice had a calming effect on the child, and he couldn't imagine doing any of this without Amber. He wasn't sure what he owed for the favor this had become. "Take a diaper from the bag next to me."

He did, ignoring the sizzle of attraction he felt when his arm brushed against her shoulder.

Amber unzipped the pink onesie pajamas and pulled each tiny foot out. Her motions were fluid, and she made it look so easy. She opened and closed the tabs on the diaper the baby already had on a couple of times as a demonstration.

"Open yours up. Figure it out. Pretend it's something mechanical and take it apart. There's not much to one of these." She leaned over and bumped his shoulder. The electricity pulsing between them from contact sent a jolt of heat rocketing through him. "My brothers' kids each seemed to have a different kind of diaper when they were this age. One needed a certain no-leak protection and another needed a specific night guard fabric."

"You mean there's more than one kind of these?" He couldn't imagine why.

"Afraid so," she said.

Rylan played around with the diaper, pretending he didn't just have the over-the-top chemistry reaction to Amber Kent. "This is pretty basic."

"Until you try to put it on a wiggly baby." Amber

was making cooing sounds, and Brooklyn seemed enraptured.

He figured he could use the distraction to change a diaper.

Removing the other diaper was easy. The rest was a bit more complicated, but with Amber's help he managed his first successful diaper change.

"Does she have any other clothes in the bag?" Amber picked up Brooklyn while he checked.

"Nope. She has what she had on yesterday." There was nothing other than formula, diapers and wipes. But that was a lot, considering the way he'd received Brooklyn. "Someone cared about her, didn't they?"

"I hope so." Amber was busy putting the pj's back on her.

"Who takes the time to write a note, pack diapers and wipes but not extra clothing?" His mind churned. "For the most part it seems that someone wanted her taken care of. I mean, there are diapers at nearly every convenience store, but her mother wanted to make sure she had the ones Brooklyn uses."

"That's a good point. It makes me think she'd been considering her options for a few days at least," Amber said.

"Brooklyn might not be my daughter. Her mother could be someone I know. I still have no idea who she could be." Whoever the woman was must know that he wouldn't take a random person's word for it that he'd fathered a child.

"Maybe she figured it would take a couple of days for the paternity test to come back and by then she'd be out of trouble and able to take her daughter back," Amber agreed. "She could've picked you because you're loyal and might be the only one she knew who could handle himself in a dangerous situation."

Which made the odds Brooklyn wasn't his child drop pretty damn drastically if he was right. But then, he'd most likely spent one or two nights with the woman in question. Wasn't exactly a recipe for knowing him, and the idea that she'd been desperate didn't sit well.

A knock sounded at the front door.

Amber gasped.

Chapter Eight

Amber didn't mean to startle the baby. She reminded herself just how much little ones picked up on the emotions and energy of everyone around them.

"It's okay, sweet princess," she soothed.

"I'll take care of whoever it is." Rylan pulled a weapon from underneath the cushion of the chair he'd been resting in earlier. The sun was up but it was still early.

Several thoughts raced through Amber's mind. Was the baby's mother back? Amber should want that, but her heart squeezed thinking about Brooklyn leaving so soon. Had the guy from yesterday returned? That was all kinds of awful, too. It could mean that Deputy Perry had been jumped or worse. She didn't want to consider the possibility that he was outside somewhere hurt because of her.

It could be good news, like Zach had found the perp who'd tried to snatch Brooklyn from Amber's arms.

Rylan checked the peephole. "I'll be right there, Zach."

He returned his weapon to its hiding place before opening the door and ushering her cousin inside.

One look at the tension lines on Zach's face and she knew something was wrong.

"You need to come back to the ranch." His lips formed a grim line. "A body was found near Rushing Creek. Female. Early to midthirties. You can ride with me if you like."

"Oh, Zach. That's terrible." Every possible worst-case scenario fought for attention in Amber's mind. "Is everyone accounted for at home?"

"Yes. Your sisters-in-law and Amy have all checked in." Zach's brows furrowed. "You gave us a scare, though. I must've called your cell ten times trying to reach you."

"My battery must've died." She regretted her word choice under the circumstances and wished she could take that last one back. She couldn't, and it wouldn't change what had happened on the ranch. It was heartbreaking.

"Everyone would rest easier if they could put eyes on you. Plus, the family wants to meet and talk about what's happening," Zach said.

Amber picked up Brooklyn and held her to her chest to keep the little girl from crying, and to give herself something to do besides give into the mounting panic attack. A woman was dead. A family was about to receive the worst possible news and suffer an unimaginable loss. Her heart ached for the victim and her family.

"Everyone on staff has been accounted for," he added. She couldn't feel much relief considering some poor soul had been killed.

"He used the same MO as the Jacobstown Hacker," Zach continued.

Her gaze bounced from Zach to Rylan. His confusion was knitted across his forehead, and she realized he must not have kept up-to-date on Jacobstown. Of course, he hadn't. He'd cut himself off from the family and, as far as she knew, hadn't been in contact with anyone recently. "Over the past few weeks, someone has been killing animals. He's specific in the way he kills them by hacking off their left paw or hoof. Up to now, the jerk had focused on animals. Now everyone's fears that he would move onto people are being realized."

"I didn't know." There was so much compassion and reverence in his voice.

"Come with me, Rylan. *Please*." She added that last part as a plea because she didn't want to leave him or the baby. Whatever had happened between him and her brother needed to be set aside, and she'd remind him of that if push came to shove. She hoped it wouldn't come to that.

"I'll get your coat," he said. She expected an argument from Rylan and was pleased when she didn't get one. There was no time. Her heart hurt for the woman at the creek. Anger burst through her that someone could get away with that on her family's property.

Rylan located her coat, which he'd hung in the closet and helped her into it. Zach stood by the door, waiting for them to get themselves and the baby ready. Amber caught him watching her as she interacted with Brooklyn, and she knew exactly what was on his mind.

Amber stopped short of the door. "We don't have a car seat for her."

"I borrowed one from Deputy Perry. He's buckling it in my SUV now." Zach opened the door and the trio followed him, with Rylan closing in from behind. His home was a half hour from the main house at the ranch. This early in the morning Zach made good time cutting across town.

Isaac was working security at the front gate. He waved them by. Amber wasted no time exiting the SUV. She tried to help unbuckle Brooklyn, but her hands shook too hard. Rylan took them in his—a move that shouldn't calm her but felt like a lifeline to sanity—and caught her gaze. He didn't say anything and yet his presence comforted her.

Amber took in a calming breath and managed to usher in Rylan's masculine scent, all pine and outdoors.

"Go on in. I'll be right there," he said.

"Okay." She couldn't imagine that it was easy for Rylan to face her family home again, and it meant the world to her that he'd come along. Strange as it might seem to an outsider since she'd only been around him and the baby a short time, they felt like part of her family, too. She told herself it was because Rylan and Will had been attached at the hip for so many years up until the summer before senior year when Rylan's mother had passed away. Then, he'd stopped coming around and Will seemed a little lost without his best friend. Amber had confronted her brother about abandoning his friend when Rylan needed him most. That had gone over about as well as sriracha on a ghost pepper.

Mitch, the eldest brother, greeted Amber in the entrance to the main living room. She could hear low chatter coming from the kitchen area. The low hum buzzed toward her, and the tone made the air heavy, like dull gray rain clouds hovering in the sky before it opened up into a show of thunder and lightning.

"The kids are at my place with Joyce. Everyone else is here, including Will," Mitch said after a hug. Joyce had been their loyal caregiver since the day the twins were born. His twins had been the first babies in the Kent family. Being the eldest brother, he probably felt more responsibility for taking care of everyone in the family. Which was most likely the reason he'd taken Amber outside to tell her when his wife had become pregnant a couple of years ago. He'd chosen his words carefully. He'd been keenly aware of what she'd been through and even time didn't seem to heal the wound of losing her child. Amber appreciated Mitch for caring. But she really didn't expect the rest of the family to stop living their lives because of her loss. It was hers.

"Does he know where I've been and who I've been helping?" She wouldn't change a thing about the past twenty-four hours; she just needed to know what she was up against.

"Yes," Mitch admitted.

Amber took in a deep breath. "Let's go."

Four brothers and three sisters-in-law sat around the large hand-carved wooden table in the massive kitchen. Seven sets of eyes landed on Amber when she walked into the room. She picked Will first. Better stare him down straightaway so he knew better than to call her out. His wife, Kelly, sat to his right. The pair had been through hell and back when Kelly was almost forced to marry a Fort Worth millionaire who was out for revenge. Amber's brother Deacon and his wife, Leah, sat across the table from the others. Leah used to work for the city of Fort Worth as a detective. She'd been targeted by a murderer posing as a copycat. In the process of investigating her case, she'd met and fallen in love with Deacon. The other couple at the table was Nate and Chelsea. She'd moved to town after an inheritance from an aunt she never knew gave her a new lease on life. But trouble soon followed, and Nate stepped up to protect Chelsea and her daughter. In the process, she and Nate had fallen in love, married and the three, plus Linda, her mother, had settled into his house on the ranch. Which left Jordan and Amber, the single siblings in an increasingly small club.

Mitch and his wife, Andrea, sat side by side. He held on to her hands, and witnessing the comfort the pair—and all the couples—seemed to provide each other struck Amber. She'd never felt hollow inside. So, where was it coming from now?

Amber expected to find disapproval in Will's eyes, but he mostly seemed concerned. He acknowledged her with a grim smile. It was most likely the weight of the situation at Rushing Creek that had him casting his gaze down and not his disappointment in her.

Zach entered the room last, and all attention went to him as Amber took a seat at the granite island toward the back of the kitchen. She couldn't be in this room anytime around the holidays without thinking just how alive it had been in past years. Maybe it was time to change that, to bring some of that love and vibrancy back to the main house. It was a point worth considering because it was so easy in life to focus on what she didn't have instead of seeing and appreciating all that she did.

"Here's what we know so far." He looked up from his notes. "This information stays inside this room, by the way."

"Goes without saying," Mitch added.

"There hasn't been confirmation of the victim's identity." Zach paused. He took caring for the people of Jacobstown seriously, and a murder in his backyard was a big hit. Especially considering the murder had happened at the family ranch.

"She was found by Lone Star Lonnie on his morning rounds. He went farther north along the creek bed chasing wild boar." Lone Star Lonnie was the foreman of KR aka Kent Ranch. "Coroner says she'd been dead for less than twelve hours. I have deputies on the scene, and Lonnie refuses to leave."

Last night was Saturday. Amber's hands fisted in her lap. This shouldn't have happened. "I realize there hasn't been confirmation, but do we have any idea who the victim might've been?"

"Lonnie did the right thing by not contaminating the crime scene. He kept his distance. Mike will text me the minute he knows something." Zach referred to Mike Travis, the county coroner.

A thought struck that Amber couldn't ignore. Could the victim be Brooklyn's mother? The baby was outside with Rylan. Was that part of the reason he'd refused to come inside? Was he thinking the same thing? It was unbearable to know any life could be cut short. Amber's heart clenched thinking that Brooklyn's mother might be the one…

"Town will want answers today about the victim, her killer and how this happened," Mitch said. He was always thinking two steps ahead, and Amber appreciated that about her brother.

"Every woman will be looking over her shoulder from now until we catch the perp," Deacon chimed in.

"I'll help in any way I can," Leah offered.

Zach thanked her.

"My office won't release information until we have all the facts," he said. "But it never hurts to issue a statement about making sure folks lock doors and keep vehicle keys with them, like we've requested in the past."

Rylan walked into the adjacent room with Brooklyn in his arms. One look at his face, and Amber could tell she'd guessed right a few minutes ago. He wore a heavy expression like he carried the weight of the world.

"If y'all will excuse me." Will stood and then walked out the back door.

"Will," Amber started, but stopped when she saw the momentary hurt darken Rylan's features. For a split second, Amber considered going after her brother. Will needed air, and he needed to accept the fact that she and Rylan were friends. Granted, what was happening felt like more than friendship to her, and she thought Rylan experienced that same heat when the two of them were in the room together. But those were facts she didn't want to examine at the moment.

Amber refocused on Will. She knew her brother well enough to realize he needed space. Rushing out there now would only hurt her cause, and both of them could end up saying words they'd regret.

"Welcome back to town, Rylan." Mitch extended the first olive branch. "I'd offer a handshake, but I can see yours are full at the moment."

"Thank you," Rylan said, and she'd never heard two more sincere words from a single soul.

"Who is that sweet little girl in your arms?" Kelly, Will's wife, asked after introducing herself.

"That's a great question." Rylan gave a quick rundown of what happened yesterday. "All we know for certain is that her name is Brooklyn."

Leah seemed to catch onto the implication that Brooklyn's mother could possibly be the victim. She introduced herself to Rylan before saying, "If you need someone to go with you to the morgue, I was a detective in a past life."

"I appreciate the offer. I'm hoping it doesn't come to that," Rylan admitted after thanking her, as well. Seeing the family, save for Will, welcome Rylan so openly caused Amber's heart to squeeze.

Andrea introduced herself, followed by Chelsea.

While introductions were being made, Amber thought back to what Rylan had told her about his sobriety. The simple truth was that he may not be able to positively ID the victim if she was Brooklyn's mother. His mind was still fuzzy about what happened that weekend, and she took to heart the seriousness in his voice when he spoke about being sober. There was so much regret and self-reproach at the possibility he'd slipped up and had a weekend binge. The fact that he hadn't had a similar one since the very early days of his sobriety struck a chord.

Zach, who had been studying his phone, walked over to Rylan. "I put the description of the man who dropped Brooklyn off at your place in the database. I flagged the file as urgent. I also just heard back from the sketch artist. She can meet this afternoon if you're still game."

Rylan was already nodding. "Of course. I want to do whatever I can to help."

"I'm probably just being Pollyanna here, but maybe we'll get lucky and the baby's mother will show up to reclaim her," Chelsea offered.

"That would be a best-case scenario for the little girl. Of course, there are legal ramifications for dropping off a baby and disappearing," Zach pointed out.

"There are no easy answers on this one." Rylan held on to the little girl, who was starting to fuss. Her gaze was locked on to Amber. From the looks of it, she found a new friend.

Mitch issued a warning look. There would be concerns from her family. They loved her and were keenly aware of her loss. Deacon was discreet, but she caught him watching her a little too intently. For now, she wanted to keep the focus on the victim and not bring up what she was doing with Rylan—other than helping an old friend after the holidays who'd been put in an impossible situation.

"It's not safe back at my house." Rylan was finally alone with Amber in the kitchen after a round of everyone wanting to meet Brooklyn. He couldn't deny the kid was cuteness times ten. She'd reeled him in almost immediately. He appreciated the kindness the Kent family showed to the little girl.

Will walking out after Rylan had come inside was a blow. He couldn't say he didn't deserve it or have it coming. It just hurt.

"After what happened last night on the ranch, I don't think it's safe anywhere." Amber blew out a defeated breath. Then she looked up at him. "I'm going with you."

"I'd argue with you but I've seen that face before," Rylan said. His cell buzzed in his pocket. He fished it out and checked the screen. "It's the doctor."

He and Amber exchanged glances. This phone call had the ability to alter that little girl's future in a big way.

"I'll hold her." Amber took the little girl, who seemed more than happy to make the switch.

Rylan answered the call and walked over to the

sink. He could see the sun bathing the yard in light. "Thanks for getting back to me so soon, Dr. Logan."

"I drew two samples, one for Zach to be locked up as evidence and the other to be sent to a lab for analysis. I had a friend open the lab and speed up the process as a favor. You deserve to know what you're dealing with, although this is unofficial word when it comes to the courts." Doc paused. "She's your daughter."

Those three words should be a gut punch. They weren't. He'd allowed that little bean to worm her way into his heart. Rylan had expected the news to hit hard. A piece of him was relieved. He tried to convince himself it was for Brooklyn's sake, that he would do a better job of protecting her than anyone else. That part was most likely true.

"Thank you, Doc," he said into the phone.

"I hope you got the news you were hoping for," Dr. Logan said.

"I appreciate the sentiment, Doc." Rylan stared out the window for a long moment, absorbing the fact that he was someone's father. And then he turned to face Amber, who'd already moved beside him, and nodded. "She's mine."

"Are you okay with the news?" she asked.

"She's a great kid. She deserves to have someone looking out for her who cares. I'm ready to be that person." Rylan meant every word. "This might not be the way I'd envisioned becoming a father. Hell,

I've never held the wife and kids fantasy. But here she is. I have every intention of doing right by her."

"Excuse me." Zach's voice came from behind them, interrupting their conversation. Based on his tone, he wasn't there for casual chatter.

Rylan turned around.

"My deputy just called. We got him. The man you described who dropped off the baby and ran yesterday morning is in custody." Zach put a hand up. "Now, I know what you're going to say and I'd probably want to do the same thing if I was in your shoes—"

"I doubt you do." Hearing the words inside his head that he was a father was about as foreign as it got. "I'm going down to your office with you."

"I wasn't about to say that you shouldn't come. I need you to identify him. All I wanted to be clear about is that you can't speak to him. You have to give me your word you'll stay on the other side of the mirror and not try to catch him in the hallway when he's being moved back and forth." Zach must've seen the tension building in Rylan's features because he kept talking. "Think of it this way. We make the right moves with this guy, and we find this girl's parents."

"Let me stop you right there, Zach. I just got a call from Dr. Logan. You'll get the official results soon enough, and they'll reveal that I'm Brooklyn's father."

Chapter Nine

After delivering the news that Rylan was Brooklyn's father, there wasn't much else that needed to be said. He had the rapt attention of everyone in the room. He turned to Amber. He'd tell her not to come with him, but he wasn't one for wasting time. She'd insist. "Are you ready?"

"Yes." The word was spoken in a firm and confident voice. No one could argue she knew what she wanted. "Can we borrow a few baby clothes before we head out?"

"We keep a few things here at the main house. I'll go grab some," Mitch said.

"While you guys wait for those, I'll get on the road. I need a five-minute head start." Zach left first.

Amber picked up the diaper bag and slid the strap over her shoulder. She looked at her family like she was daring one of them to speak. Will, the one person Rylan wanted to speak to the most, was outside somewhere, most likely in the barn. Work did a lot of good to clear the mind. It was also a great outlet for anger, an emotion Rylan understood all too well.

"Thank you for your hospitality." Rylan meant those words.

Mitch returned with a few items that he handed to Amber. He walked over and put his hand on Rylan's shoulder. "It took a lot to show up here, Rylan. You always were like family. If you need anything come back any—"

"Thank you, but I doubt everyone shares that sentiment." He motioned toward the barn.

"You know Will. He needs a minute. But he'll come around." Mitch set his jaw, looking confident in those words.

"Some people don't deserve forgiveness," Rylan said to Mitch.

"That's where you're wrong. Everyone does." Mitch squeezed Rylan's shoulder before leaning in close to his ear. "She'd kill me if she knew I said anything. But take it easy with her."

Rylan issued a grunt. "Amber can—"

"Hear me out," Mitch interrupted. "She probably didn't tell you but she was married before."

"Amber?" She never said anything about a husband. Why did it hit him so hard that she'd kept something so big a secret?

"It didn't go well for her. There was a child involved and—"

Those words hit like another rogue wave. It was

starting to make sense why the family seemed so
concerned when she'd taken Brooklyn in her arms.
Anyone could see those two were natural together.
Had she been married to a man who'd had a child
in a previous relationship? It made sense as to why
she'd been so cautious with him.

"Based on your expression I'm guessing you had
no clue about either one of those things," Mitch said.

"Not a one." Rylan was still trying to absorb the
first of the two revelations.

"I shouldn't have said anything. Those are not
my secrets to share. I just don't want to see her heart
ripped out—"

"You're trying to protect her."

Amber walked into the kitchen. She froze when
she saw the two of them in intimate conversation.
She balled a fist and planted it on her hip. "What's
going on in here?"

"We were just talking," Rylan started, but she
grunted.

"I figured that much out. You plan on telling me
what you were talking about?" she asked.

"We can talk on the way over to Zach's office.
Did you pick up your phone charger?" Rylan hoped
the distraction would work.

It seemed to when she spun around and walked
out of the room. She returned a few minutes later
looking more than ready to go.

"Zach was our ride," Rylan pointed out. And he'd left minutes ago.

"I have more than one vehicle, Rylan. And I keep a car seat in the back of my small sport utility." Amber's gaze moved from Mitch to Rylan. "What were the two of you talking about?"

"I was just giving Rylan some kid advice," Mitch said, sidestepping the question.

"You sure that's all?" Amber asked her brother.

"I told him to be cautious with you and that if he hurt you I'd be on his doorstep." He walked over and put his hands on her shoulders.

"You know I'm a big girl, Mitch. I appreciate you having my back, but I'm capable of fighting my own battles," she said.

"Maybe I think you shouldn't have to fight anyone anymore." Mitch pulled her into a bear hug. "Love you, sis."

"I know you do." Amber returned the hug cautiously. "But we've gotta go."

Rylan took the lead, walking toward the door. Part of him needed to know what had happened to her. He wanted, no needed to know if what Mitch said had anything to do with the seriousness in her eyes. Years ago, she'd been all spunk and spark and fire. Her heart was bigger and more open than the Texas sky. And he could still see those qualities in her, but some of that spark had dimmed and he wondered how much it had to do with her ex, with having a child taken away from her.

Thinking about anyone hurting Amber caused a fire bolt to swirl through Rylan.

Leah stopped them at the front door. "Have you guys considered leaving the baby here until you figure out what's going on at Zach's office? We have plenty of qualified family members here to take care of her, and there are lots of kiddos on the ranch. I doubt anyone would notice one more."

Before Rylan could form an argument, Amber answered for him.

"She'll be safer with us, and Rylan wouldn't be able to concentrate if she's away from him," she said. She was right, and he was surprised that she could read him so well. "But we're grateful for the offer."

"Let us know if that changes. Any one of us could come pick her up at Zach's office if the situation drags on or gets too tense." Deacon moved beside his wife, nodding his agreement with what she said. He put his arm around her, and Rylan was struck at how happy they seemed.

"Thank you," Rylan said, and he meant it for both of them.

Amber added an extra blanket over the baby. Rylan opened the door for Amber, who walked outside and into the brisk afternoon air. She shivered. "It's gotten even colder."

A blanket of gray clouds covered the sky, making it feel later in the day than it was.

Amber handed him the keys to her small sport utility after helping to buckle Brooklyn into her car seat. She stopped long enough to ask, "What did Mitch really say to you in the house?"

"Enough to make me curious about your past," he admitted before taking the proffered keys and moving to the driver's seat.

Amber put some muscle into closing her door after getting inside. "Did he tell you that I was married?"

"Yes. But that's all. He said it was a long time ago." Rylan turned the key in the ignition, and the engine hummed to life. He put the gearshift in Reverse.

"What else did he say?" she demanded, and her voice was a study in calm. He couldn't decide if that was good or bad.

There was no point beating around the bush, and he didn't like the idea of hiding information from her, so he came out with it. "Did your husband have a kid?"

"*I* had a child, Rylan. He was stillborn—"

"I'm so sorry, Amber. It's none of my business. You don't have to talk about it if you don't want to." His heart fisted in his chest thinking about the pain she must've endured as he pulled off the drive and put the transmission in Park.

He turned to her as she stared out the front windshield. "I was out of line bringing it up, Amber. And so was Mitch. He never should've stirred that pot."

"That's the thing, Rylan. I never talk about him. My family always tiptoes around the subject and I get it. They're afraid of dredging up the past, and I love the fact that they want to protect me. From what I can see that can be rare in families, and I wish more people had loved ones who would do just about anything for them." She paused and he let her catch her breath as a few tears rolled down her cheeks. "But I'm done talking about this for now. We have a little girl in the back seat who needs all of our attention."

"When you're ready to keep going, I'm here." A dozen questions fired off in his mind. This wasn't the time for any of them. He couldn't help but wonder if losing a baby was what caused the sadness in her eyes. It was a flash, and he'd almost missed it a few times already. There was another emotion present when she held Brooklyn that made sense to him now.

"That means a lot to me, Rylan."

She turned to face him, and he leaned over the armrest to brush his fingertips across her cheek. "I wish there was something I could say or do that could take that pain away from your eyes, Amber."

"No one can take that away, Rylan. But you can do something," she said.

"Name it. I'll do anything." He meant it, too.

"Kiss me."

"THAT'S NOT A GOOD IDEA," Rylan said, but there was no conviction in his tone.

She leaned toward him, and they were so close she could breathe the same air. His masculine scent filled her senses, destroying her ability to think clearly. "No. It's not. But it's too late for me."

With that, he dipped his head and claimed her mouth. She parted her lips for him and teased his tongue inside. For something that should be avoided at all cost, kissing Rylan sure felt right in the moment.

But then she'd thought about the one kiss they'd shared in high school more times than she cared to admit. She could be real about it. He'd most likely been drinking. In fact, back then she thought she tasted alcohol on his breath. When she'd accused him of kissing her because he was drunk, he'd laughed and told her he kissed her because he realized how beautiful she was. That night at the bunkhouse, where she'd often gone to clear her thoughts, he'd looked at her like it was the first time he'd really seen her. She'd changed over the summer and had grown two inches, to her current height.

And ever since he opened the door yesterday, she'd been wanting him to kiss her again to see if it would be as magical as it felt that night.

Rylan's hands came up to cup her face, and she brought hers up to get lost in his thick dark hair.

She'd never experienced so much passion in a kiss

with any other man, not even the one she'd been married to.

The skill with which Rylan kissed Amber caused her mind to snap to other pleasures she figured he'd mastered, as well. She could only imagine the sparks that would fly in the bedroom based on the heat she was experiencing right then.

The baby cooed in the back seat, breaking into the moment.

Amber pulled back first, and he stopped her with his hands. He looked into her eyes, and it felt like he was looking right through her.

"Damn," he said under his breath. That one word was about the sexiest thing Amber had heard.

She laughed at herself and he cocked an eyebrow.

"That's not a response I'm used to in situations like this," he said, but then he smiled, too.

"I don't doubt you have a lot of experience in situations like this, Rylan Anderson," she quipped.

"That might be true. But none have ever felt like this."

Now it was her turn to say the word *damn*.

With that, he turned his attention back to the road ahead. He navigated back onto the driveway and onto the farm road.

Amber didn't ask how long Rylan planned to stick around. Staying in one place seemed to suffocate Rylan once he turned eighteen. He'd never been good at holding on to a possession for more than a few months. The pattern was always the same. He'd get a new motorcycle, and it would be all the rage for a few weeks. He'd tire of it and sell it only to buy a four-wheeler a few days later. The only certainty was that he'd get bored with his latest toy and move onto something *or someone* else. She figured some people didn't stick. They moved in and out of cities, jobs, lives. She would do well to remember that, because he'd moved out of hers once already. An annoying little voice reminded her that he'd come back to Jacobstown and that technically he didn't *leave* her.

Having a daughter would change him but nothing would tame him. He'd always walked the edge. He didn't grow up with money. He'd worked for every penny. But that didn't mean he spent it wisely. At least back then. She remembered the time he bought an old Jeep and then got bored with it before he was finished paying for it and lost money on the deal. It wasn't the money she worried about. Young people didn't have the same understanding of finances that someone with real responsibilities did. It was his attention span that bothered her.

Thick gray clouds rolled across the sky. Amber had a bad feeling in the pit of her stomach.

Luckily, Brooklyn had a full stomach. She was cooing happily by herself in the back seat. The two-lane farm road leading away from the ranch was empty at this hour on a Sunday. The temperature was dropping. The cold front was blowing through, and the temperature had dropped into the thirties. At least the temperature was above freezing and it was dry outside.

The conditions threatened to worsen, but the best thing about Texas weather was that it changed on a dime. People always said if someone didn't like the weather, all they had to do was stick around for five minutes and it would change. And if not five minutes, then a couple of days before the sun would shine and the days would warm up again.

Rylan cursed as he checked the rearview mirror. An all-black sporty sedan roared up behind them. There were no markings on the vehicle. Amber took note of the plate. "I think we should keep an eye on this guy."

"Maybe we should turn around and head back to the ranch where we have backup," Rylan said. They'd driven halfway to Zach's office.

Amber briefly thought about making a call for help. She'd charged her cell enough at the house to be able to make a call. This far away who would be able to get to them? Amber's heart galloped. Trees lined both sides of the road. Turning around was their safest, and only bet. She studied the car behind them. "It almost looks like an unmarked vehicle."

"Why would law enforcement be out here on this farm road?" Rylan made a good point.

"Wish I knew." She glanced back at the sedan.

"This doesn't feel right to me, Rylan. We rarely ever have another agency here in town that Zach doesn't know about. Maybe we should give him a call just to check in with him."

"That's probably smart," Rylan said.

Amber called her cousin, who picked up on the first ring. "We have a suspicious vehicle on our tail and Brooklyn is with us. Do you know anything about outside law enforcement being in the area?"

"I haven't heard a word. That doesn't mean another agency couldn't be involved, especially if Brooklyn was taken across state lines. We have no idea what we're truly dealing with, and I can't speak for another office," Zach stated. "What does the vehicle look like?"

She described it.

"What about the license plate? Maybe I can run it through the database and get a hit," he offered before seeming to think better of it and adding, "Although, any undercover operation would be blocked."

"It's worth a try." Amber chanced a glance behind.

Everything was quiet for a few seconds save for the sound of tires on the road and the unaware baby in the back.

"While I'm waiting to see if we get a hit, which vehicle is Rylan driving?"

"We're in my small SUV."

"Is that the one you take on cattle runs sometimes?" Most cattle ranchers used ATVs or pickup trucks and not horses like her family usually did. It was a tradition her father had started when they were young, and everyone kept it up most of the time.

"Yes."

"Have your weapon at the ready just in case there's trouble." She located her SIG Sauer in the glove compartment. Granted, it was normally her brothers going up against dangerous poachers, but she knew how to protect herself and she, like everyone else, carried anytime she went out on the property. A coyote could be lurking behind any tree or bush. Wild hogs were mean creatures, not to mention dangerous. And then there were poachers. She'd encountered the first two more times than she cared to count. She'd been spared the latter so far.

"I have DPS on the line. I need to put you on hold." Zach waited for acknowledgment, which she gave.

A grin lifted one side of Rylan's mouth. "I'd ask if you know what to do with that SIG, but I know better. Remember the time you shot a hole in my favorite ballcap?"

She couldn't help but laugh at the memory.

"You were just lucky it wasn't on your head at the time," she quipped, grateful for the momentary break in tension.

But then the sports sedan sped up toward the bumper.

"What do we do here, Rylan? What's our move?"

Chapter Ten

Lights swirled from the black sedan behind them. Amber wished Zach would come back on the line so he could tell them what to do.

"Anyone comes at us with a weapon we protect ourselves." Rylan pulled onto the shoulder of the two-lane road as he surveyed the landscape.

"This is bad," she said.

"If that little bean wasn't in the back seat and you weren't here, this would be right up my alley," he stated with one of those devastating smiles that was all Rylan. She tried to convince herself that it was the heat in the moment that sent a rocket of electricity shooting through her, and not the fact that she had a very real *and growing* attraction to the man in the driver's seat. "As it is, I have to consider both of you."

"Thanks for the confidence in my shot." Amber snorted.

"I just mean that if either of you got hurt because of me I'd never forgive myself. So, I can't be my usual self on a mission." His voice dipped when he spoke those words aloud. It always had a deep, musical quality that she could listen to all day. His voice poured over her like Amaretto over ice cream, melting her insides as it washed through her.

He covered her hand with his, and electricity pulsed through her. It was his masculine and all-male presence that did that to her, made her want things she knew better than to think about.

"I can take Brooklyn and run into the woods. No one would know this area better than me, and that would give you time to handle these guys on your own," she said.

The lights continued to swirl, but the driver didn't exit his vehicle. A pickup truck did come speeding up on the road in front of them, barreling toward them.

"Whatever happens next, I'm glad you came back, Rylan," she admitted. She wanted, no *needed* him to know that.

"Don't count me out yet, Kent," he countered with the sexy little smirk that dented the corner of his cheek. He was in his element.

A man in what looked like a state trooper uniform exited the vehicle. His tan uniform and hat seemed authentic.

"Something feels off, but I can't quite put my finger on it," Amber said.

"One Minute" Survey

You get up to **FOUR** books <u>and</u> TWO Mystery Gifts...

YOU pick your books –
WE pay for everything.
You get up to FOUR new books and TWO Mystery Gifts,
absolutely FREE!
Total retail value: Over $20!

Dear Reader,

Your opinions are important to us. So if you'll participate in our fast and free "One Minute" Survey, **YOU** can pick up to four wonderful books that **WE** pay for!

As a leading publisher of women's fiction, we'd love to hear from you. That's why we promise to reward you for completing our survey.

IMPORTANT: Please complete the survey and return it. We'll send your Free Books and Free Mystery Gifts right away. **And we pay for shipping and handling too!** *We pay for EVERYTHING!*

Try **Harlequin® Romantic Suspense** books featuring heart-racing page-turners with unexpected plot twists and irresistible chemistry that will keep you guessing to the very end.

Try **Harlequin Intrigue® Larger-Print** books featuring action-packed stories that will keep you on the edge of your seat. Solve the crime and deliver justice at all costs.

Or TRY BOTH!

Thank you again for participating in our "One Minute" Survey. It really takes just a minute (or less) to complete the survey… and your free books and gifts will be well worth it!

Sincerely,

Pam Powers

Pam Powers
for Reader Service

www.ReaderService.com

"One Minute" Survey

GET YOUR FREE BOOKS AND FREE GIFTS!

✓ Complete this Survey   ✓ Return this survey

1 Do you try to find time to read every day?
☐ YES   ☐ NO

2 Do you prefer stories with suspenseful storylines?
☐ YES   ☐ NO

3 Do you enjoy having books delivered to your home?
☐ YES   ☐ NO

4 Do you find a Larger Print size easier on your eyes?
☐ YES   ☐ NO

YES! I have completed the above "One Minute" Survey. Please send me my Free Books and Free Mystery Gifts (worth over $20 retail). I understand that I am under no obligation to buy anything, as explained on the back of this card.

☐ I prefer Harlequin®
Romantic Suspense
240/340 HDL GNUS

☐ I prefer Harlequin
Intrigue® Larger Print
199/399 HDL GNUS

☐ I prefer BOTH
240/340 & 199/399
HDL GNWG

FIRST NAME

LAST NAME

ADDRESS

APT.#

CITY

STATE/PROV.

ZIP/POSTAL CODE

Offer limited to one per household and not applicable to series that subscriber is currently receiving. **Your Privacy**—The Reader Service is committed to protecting your privacy. Our Privacy Policy is available online at www.ReaderService.com or upon request from the Reader Service. We make a portion of our mailing list available to reputable third parties that offer products we believe may interest you. If you prefer that we not exchange your name with third parties, or if you wish to clarify or modify your communication preferences, please visit us at www.ReaderService.com/consumerschoice or write to us at Reader Service Preference Service, P.O. Box 9062, Buffalo, NY 14240-9062. Include your complete name and address.

RS/HI-520-OM20

▶ DETACH AND MAIL CARD TODAY!

© 2019 HARLEQUIN ENTERPRISES ULC and ® are trademarks owned by Harlequin Enterprises ULC. Printed in the U.S.A.

The truck was getting closer as the officer walked toward them.

"Wouldn't he wait? I mean why get out of his vehicle on a two-lane road while a truck is steaming toward us?" Rylan had good questions.

"I'm concerned about this, Rylan." She scanned the officer and it struck her. "Zach never makes a traffic stop without his hand on the butt of his gun, in case of trouble. I've never seen any officer just walk up like this. Also, notice how much is missing from his belt?"

Rylan muttered the same curse she was thinking. Turning the steering wheel a hard left, he mashed the gas pedal. "Take the safety off and get ready to shoot if he so much as looks like he's about to pull his weapon and fire."

The tires peeled out as Rylan banked a U-turn and then navigated the small sport utility on the shoulder and past the black sedan.

"I sure hope you have a plan that doesn't involve getting rammed in the bumper by a pickup truck that weighs far more than my car." She braced for impact, and her thoughts immediately snapped to the little girl in the back seat. Even in a car seat she could be hurt by an impact.

The black sedan's engine revved, and then the vehicle spun around to follow them.

Rylan's reflexes were spot-on as he shifted to

the right and swerved so that the pickup missed the bumper.

Zach returned to the line, and Amber gave her cousin the quick rundown and told him they were headed back toward the ranch with two vehicles on their tail. She ended the call. "He promised to send the closest deputy. He's also calling my brothers, so help should be here in a few minutes."

Rylan pushed the SUV as fast as it could go, outmaneuvering the other pursuing vehicles, and she could see why he was the best at what he did. His confidence was earned. She and the baby were handicaps that he wasn't used to accounting for.

Amber was ready with her SIG, but she really didn't want to get a shooting match started. There was no telling where a stray bullet might end up, and she wouldn't risk Brooklyn's safety.

The road zigzagged ahead, and Rylan drove like an Indy driver on a hot track. He checked the rearview mirror a couple of times before she could visibly see tension leaving his shoulders as the other vehicles moved out of sight.

"They're gone. But I have bad news. You're stuck with me until this whole situation is settled."

"I get that we'll have to hide, but where can we go with an infant?" Traveling with a child wouldn't be easy. If Brooklyn cried at the wrong time, it could be game over. Even Amber realized that.

"Call Mitch. Let him know what just happened. Security needs to be made aware of another threat to the ranch. We can't take anyone's safety for granted." He was right.

The phone call home was short. She relayed the details. Everyone was already on high alert due to the murder that had happened last night. All Amber could think about was getting to her cousin's office and hearing what the mystery man who'd dropped off Brooklyn had to say. Certainly, he'd be able to describe the woman who handed over the baby, and that might jar Rylan's memory. Would she match the victim?

Right now, they had little to go on, and Rylan didn't seem able to remember being with Brooklyn's mother, or any other woman, during that time frame. He'd insisted that alcohol likely played a role in his memory loss, but after being around him she highly doubted that had happened. They would find another explanation if they looked hard enough. She believed that with her whole heart. "Do you think the guys who were following us will expect us to show up at the ranch? They could be circling back."

"I know a back way to Zach's office from here." Rylan made a couple of turns that would have them doubling back. His gaze was intense on the stretch of road in front of them. "I'm sorry I got you involved in this, Amber. I truly am."

"You didn't do anything on purpose." How could he have known how this would all shake out?

"I have no idea what Brooklyn's mother got herself into, but this isn't good and I'd bet anything now she got involved in something illegal." He gripped the steering wheel. That steel resolve was in his voice, but she didn't like the undercurrent of resignation that she picked up on, too.

"We'll find out soon enough. This guy at Zach's office will lead us to Brooklyn's mother—"

"Who might not still be alive," he stated.

"We can't think like that until we know for certain. I'm sure once you hear a description of her it'll all come back. We'll find her and figure out what made her leave this beautiful little girl and take off. I mean, she must've cared about her daughter because she did find a way to leave her with her father," Amber stated.

"What if—" He stopped himself. "No. Never mind."

"Go ahead. Say what you're thinking," she urged.

"I wasn't in a good place that weekend if I had a drink, Amber. There's a chance her description won't ring any bells. And then what? I've put you in danger for nothing." It wasn't exactly defeat in his voice that she heard, but she didn't like where this was going.

"If this guy gives us good information and if it clicks who he's talking about right away, then great. We still have to locate her, and from what I can gather so far, she seems to be in pretty big trouble.

Look at that angel in the back seat. She's been well taken care of for three months. Her mother wouldn't do that if she didn't love her. And anyone who takes that good care of her baby can't be all bad. Maybe she got herself in a tough spot and went to the wrong people for help." Amber could only hope her words were sinking in. "It'll be okay. You'll see. This'll all be over soon, and you can start figuring out your next move. You can look forward to getting to know your daughter, Rylan. What could be better than that?"

Amber wiped away an unexpected tear as Rylan navigated into the parking lot of Zach's office, and then parked in a spot close to the front door.

THE SEDAN AND the pickup truck were gone for now. That most likely meant the drivers were on a scouting mission. Experience had taught Rylan that the men would return, ready to strike next time. They'd be better prepared. That was the only explanation for why they didn't shoot. Which led him to the conclusion that someone wanted Brooklyn.

They'd have to kill him to get to her. And based on the protective look on Amber's face as he walked beside her into her cousin's office, the same went for her.

Rylan had had bad days in his life. Hell, most of them could be considered bad once his mother passed away. There was something about that little girl in Amber's arms that gave him a sense of hope. He chalked it up to the innocence children brought, the new perspective on life. Brooklyn was a good baby, which most likely meant she'd been well cared for up to this point. Her whole life was ahead of her.

A thought struck Rylan as he held the door open for Amber. What if her mother never turned up? Or, worse, what if she turned out to be the victim? What if the thing she'd gotten herself into caused her to lose her life? Other thoughts joined. What if she was sick? What if giving Brooklyn to him was a last-ditch effort to give the baby a chance at life?

All those thoughts amounted to a hill of beans when it came to thinking about anything happening to that little girl. Was there a court in the world that would take her away from him? He hoped the hell not. Because he was all-in when it came to Brooklyn from now on. It was a foreign feeling to him. He hadn't felt like he belonged to something bigger than himself in too long.

Shoving those thoughts aside, he entered Zach's office.

"We're going down the hall." Zach pushed off his desk, stood and focused on Amber. "There were no hits on the vehicles you described."

"They'll be back," Rylan stated.

"We'll be ready." Zach's resolve almost had Rylan believing the man could handle whatever entered his county. But Rylan didn't have time for false hope. This was bigger than Zach and his deputies. Besides, they had a murder to investigate. "But first, follow me."

Rylan put his hand on the small of Amber's back and ignored the heat pulsing through his fingertips from the contact. This wasn't the time to notice the attraction sizzling between them or think about the kiss they'd shared. Or the fact that he'd never experienced a pull this strong to any other woman.

He forced the thoughts to the back of his mind and refocused on the man who started all this. The blond.

The small room down the hallway from Zach's office had low lighting, no doubt because of the one-way mirror. The room itself wasn't much bigger than a walk-in closet. The space on the other side of the mirror doubled in size. There was a table and two chairs placed opposite each other. The white tile seemed sterile and like what Rylan would find in a hospital hallway. The walls were barren and gray. The only wall decoration visible to Rylan was an analog wall clock. It was circular, about a foot in diameter with large black numbers. The timepiece hung above the only door in and out of the space.

Everything about the room was meant to make someone uncomfortable. It was damn smart because Rylan was uncomfortable looking inside.

The door opened and a deputy walked in with a

man in cuffs shuffling behind him. Rylan recognized the man immediately as the one from yesterday, and he felt the tension stiffen his shoulders. He rolled them back to loosen the knots, but it didn't do any good.

"Is it him?" Amber was studying Rylan, and he figured she already knew the answer to that question.

"He's the one." Those three words confirmed what she clearly had already guessed.

The man wore a camouflage hunting jacket, blue jeans and boots. He was much shorter than Rylan, not six feet tall if he had to venture a guess.

Deputy Perry instructed the suspect to sit. From opposite the table his shoulders were square with Rylan, which was good. The man was close enough for Rylan to see clearly. The interview room was small, and he figured it was designed that way on purpose.

He felt Amber move beside him with the baby in her arms.

The deputy's back was to them. "State your name."

"Chester Hunter III, but my friends call me Chess." Chess sat on the edge of the seat as he wiped his palms on his thighs. Rylan could only guess the man had sweaty palms. Chess displayed other signs of nervousness. Sweat beaded on his forehead, and he blinked at a rapid pace. He spoke a little too fast, and his voice was a higher pitch than Rylan remembered.

Zach opened the door and popped his head in

the viewing room. He looked at Rylan. "Can I get a positive ID?"

"I'm certain it was him," Rylan responded.

"He's not denying his involvement. The deputy asked him to wait to give a statement until I could make it in." Zach put a hand on Rylan's shoulder. "Let's hope we get the answers we're looking for."

"Do you live in Jacobstown?" Deputy Perry continued.

"No, sir. I'm from Bremmer City." Bremmer City was to the south of Jacobstown. Rylan had done some partying there in his youth before signing up for the military and righting his life.

"Did you bring a child to a residence in Jacobstown yesterday?" Deputy Perry jotted down a couple of notes. His posture was the opposite of Chess's. The deputy sat comfortably in the metal and plastic chair. His feet were apart, and he leaned forward on the table in between him and Chess.

"Yes, sir." Chess's right leg started shaking. The man looked to be in his late twenties.

"What's your occupation?" Perry asked.

"Mill worker," Chess replied. "I work for my father's construction company. He builds custom homes."

Perry asked a few follow-up questions.

"Can you describe the child in question?" Fact-checking was a routine part of any investigation.

"She was a little girl. Small enough to fit into one of those carriers you see people with all the time. Her hair was black, curly." He'd gone from a shaking leg to tapping the toe of his boot against the tile floor. "She was a cute kid."

"How old was she?" The deputy's voice was a study in calm. He was almost conspiratorial.

"I don't have enough experience with kids to tell. All I know is she was young enough and small enough to fit into the carrier." The words came out rushed.

"Did she have anything else with her?" Again, the deputy was confirming facts.

"Yeah. She had a diaper bag."

"Can you tell me how you came to be in possession of the child?" Rylan's ears perked up.

"Of course. I was pumping gas at the 401, the one by the Pig's Ear down on farm road 26. That's the one I always go to because gas is always cheaper than by the interstate." He blinked up at the deputy like competing gas prices were common knowledge.

The deputy nodded.

"So, I'm pumping gas when a woman holding a baby in a carrier comes up to me. She looked scared and her eyes were saucers, like a cornered animal's. She comes up to me and starts begging me to help her out. I'm looking all around expecting someone to charge up to us, or something—"

"Can you describe her?" Deputy Perry asked.

Rylan leaned toward the glass and listened.

"She was pretty. Her hair and eyes were brown, like coffee beans. She stood about yay high." He held his right hand up to his chin, which would make her about five feet five inches.

Rylan drew a blank.

The deputy scribbled more notes. "Can you describe what she was wearing?"

"Yeah. She had on some kind of shirt with jeans. The shirt was short-sleeved. Oh, and flip-flops. I noticed because I thought it was weird she wasn't wearing a coat or real shoes since it was so cold out." His gaze was fixed but there was nothing on the walls to stare at, and it was one of those blank stares like when someone recalled facts.

To Rylan's thinking, the guy seemed legitimate. He was definitely the man from the other day. There was no question. Rylan had wondered if Chess was involved. Based on his reactions and what he said so far, there was nothing to make Rylan believe that was true.

Deputy Perry glanced up. "Did you say flip-flops?"

"I thought that was weird, too," Chess stated. "The kid was bundled up, though. She had a warm blanket over her and a hat on."

Flip-flops on a frigid day. No coat. The mystery woman was in a hurry, which supported the idea that she'd been in grave danger. Could she be from the area?

Chess's statement made Rylan think the mystery woman had found out at the last minute that someone was coming for her or the baby. The last thought struck a chord. Was the mystery woman in trouble herself and trying to off-load the baby, or was someone after Brooklyn instead?

The fact that someone was *still* after the little girl—his daughter—gave him the strong impression she was the target. Had they gotten to Brooklyn's mother? Had she disappeared in time, afraid to show up while the men chasing her were in town?

There were more questions than answers in this case.

Amber looked to Rylan expectantly.

He shook his head. "I don't know who she is."

"Did she have any distinguishing marks? Scars? Birthmarks? Tattoos?" Deputy Perry returned his focus to the notepad as he scribbled.

"Not that I can think of." Chess returned his focus to the spot it had been before. And then his face twisted. "You know, now that you mention it she did have a birthmark on her neck. It was low, close to her collarbone. On her left side because facing me it was on the right."

That struck a chord. A vague memory tried to take shape in Rylan's mind, but it was still a blur. He'd been running on no sleep for weeks during a mission in Kandahar. And then he'd gone to San Antonio for the last three months where he'd remained until getting his papers and moving to Jacobstown.

There was a time in his life when finding out he'd had a child after a weekend of partying wouldn't have surprised him. Granted, he wouldn't be proud of himself. But he wouldn't be shocked, either.

Looking back, shame for the way he'd handled his stress, his life, engulfed him like an out-of-control forest fire. Now that his head was clear, he could acknowledge that he'd used alcohol to deal with the stress of losing his mother before he was out of high school. He'd worked hard and partied even harder until that last time when he was so out of it he caught the Willows' crops on fire. He'd been so out of it that he'd almost died. It was a wake-up call. After that, he realized he needed to deal with his pent-up emotions in a healthier manner. Truth of the matter was that he'd wanted to be a better man. The desire had spread like a wildfire after Will had lied in order to protect Rylan.

Becoming sober hadn't been easy. He'd attacked it like everything in his life. He'd gone all-in. He'd realized that he needed to open up and talk, let people in rather than hold everything inside. He'd started talking after that instead of ignoring his pain and little by little was able to let the past go.

Admitting he'd needed help went against everything inside him as a soldier who'd been trained to rely on himself and take care of everyone else around him. Until he realized it made him far more of a man to own up to his mistakes, to his weaknesses. The hardest damn thing had been taking an honest look in the mirror.

Rylan would never be free of the shame, the guilt until he made things right in Jacobstown. He had two apologies left to make. One to the Willow family and the other to Will Kent. He owed the Willows retribution. But how did he repay Will? How did he square with the man who'd stepped up and blamed his own negligence for the fire that devoured the Willows' crops and almost their livelihood?

Mr. and Mrs. Kent had stepped in to get the Willows back on their feet. He couldn't apologize to them or thank them for what they'd done. But he owed the Kent family. He sure as hell wasn't repaying them by getting Amber mixed up in his life. That made two Kents who should know better than to put their trust in Rylan.

Chapter Eleven

Amber stared at the one-way mirror. Hearing details about a woman Rylan had had a fling with shouldn't have this effect on her. So, why did it?

One kiss, no matter how electric it had been, did not a relationship make. Besides, getting involved with Rylan beyond friendship would be a mistake. He seemed to realize it as much as she did.

She bounced Brooklyn on her hip, reminding herself that she had no claim on Rylan. The two were friends and he'd come to her for help, not for a relationship. Was there chemistry between them? She'd be a fool to deny it. They'd always been able to laugh and joke around when they were younger. She'd always felt a little spark whenever Rylan was over. That spark had ignited into a full-blown attraction.

And how smart was that on her part?

Pretty damn stupid.

Rylan might have a child—and she had no doubt this little girl would be the one thing that Rylan would stick to—but that didn't change who he was. He would always move on. Those words, that honesty shouldn't feel like a knife wound to her chest.

Amber needed to create a little emotional distance. She took a step away from him as she examined the face of the man being questioned. Strange that he lived one town over but she had no idea who he was. It seemed like everyone knew each other in Jacobstown, but that wasn't exactly true. People moved in and out without being known.

Zach entered the viewing room. "How's it going in here?"

She knew what he was really asking. *Was any of this ringing a bell?*

"Not as well as I would like," Rylan responded.

"The coroner is sending over pictures of the victim in the hopes of a positive ID." Zach's voice held the respect of a deacon during Sunday morning church service.

Amber's heart went out to the little girl in her arms. It made sense that her mother would've given her to someone else if she suspected something was about to happen. Had her mother seen death coming? Was that why she'd made a bold move in making sure the child got to Rylan?

It was strange that Brooklyn's mother could be somehow tied to the Jacobstown Hacker. Or maybe she wasn't. Amber leaned toward Rylan and asked,

"What do you think the odds of her mother being connected to the Jacobstown Hacker are?"

"I thought about that, too. Maybe she was an innocent victim of his, the perfect opportunity for him to finally strike." Rylan folded his arms across his broad chest.

Amber hugged Brooklyn a little closer to her. She couldn't imagine growing up without a mother. It was difficult enough to lose a mother as an adult. But as a child? Amber was even more grateful for the time she had with hers.

An argument could be made that Brooklyn's mother wasn't at the top of her game. She'd obviously gotten herself into some kind of trouble. She knew to stash her child away safely. Now that the paternity test had come back, it was certain that Rylan was the child's father.

What could Brooklyn's mother have possibly gotten herself into that could force her to hide her daughter? Coming to Jacobstown must've been a last-ditch effort. But showing up in flip-flops in late January, not wearing a coat?

Granted, it appeared as though she wasn't here on her own accord. She'd wrapped up the child in blankets and a hat before handing her off to a stranger and, what? Hoped for the best? That screamed of desperation. The woman didn't take time to put her own coat on.

The interview in the next room continued, and Amber realized she'd spaced out for a second.

"Did you ask the woman with the baby her name?" Deputy Perry continued.

"No. I didn't really think to at the time—"

"A woman thrusts her child at you and you weren't the least bit curious about her background?" Perry lifted a brow.

"It wasn't like that. She came up to me and begged me to take her baby. She said she needed help, but I told her to go inside the convenience store and tell the clerk. I told her to call the sheriff but—" His words came out faster this time. He'd already been rushing his speech, but he shifted in his seat and put his hands up to his face. "She said she couldn't involve the sheriff. Or something along those lines. I'd finished pumping my gas and was putting the nozzle back in the receptor by then. My first thought was that she was on something, but as she talked I realized she was scared."

"And what was your response?" There was no sound of judgment in the deputy's voice. Amber was too emotional to work in law enforcement. The thought of a man refusing to help someone in need riled her up too much. She'd never be so diplomatic. But then, that's probably one of many reasons she was a cattle rancher and didn't wear a badge.

"My mind immediately snapped to someone abusing her. That's when I looked for signs," he stated.

"And did you find any?" Deputy Perry spun the pen between his fingers as he waited for a response.

"That's when I saw the birthmark. No bruising, though. But that doesn't mean it wasn't somewhere on her body. She rattled off an address and said she needed to get the baby there ASAP." He paused for a beat. "She also said to make sure I wasn't followed."

"How did you respond to her?"

"I told her that I couldn't help her. She needed to go to the law." He flashed his eyes at the deputy. "I had a cousin who got shot for trying to help a friend of his who was in an argument with her boyfriend. I don't stick my nose where it doesn't belong."

Domestic violence was a serious issue. Amber had heard from Zach countless times those calls were the most dangerous. Domestic violence calls and traffic stops ranked up there as the most threatening to officers.

Still. Every one of Amber's brothers would stop to help any person in need. There'd be no question. She could tell by the way Rylan tensed that he would've done the same. That was his personality. He might be the type to move around and never settle in one place for long but he wouldn't turn down anyone who asked him for a hand.

"What happened next?" Deputy Perry kept the interview on target.

"She got a panicked look. Started looking from side

to side like someone might jump out from behind the gas pump. I'd finished my business so I told her that I had to go inside and pay. I told her to come with me and call someone. That's when she took off running." He paused another beat. "I figured that was the last I'd see of her or her baby. But when my back was turned she sneaked the baby in the driver's seat and took off."

"How'd you remember the address?" Perry made a good point.

"Easy. My mom moved out that way when she and my pops divorced. I'd been over there more than a few times to visit. Mom used to live next door to Mrs. Parker." Chess seemed satisfied with himself for the answer.

Amber turned to face Zach. "Any chance he could be *him*?"

"He would've been the last one to see her alive if the victim turns out to be Brooklyn's mother, which makes him our top suspect," Zach stated. "And he just admitted to being familiar with the area."

"I picked up on that, too." A shiver raced down Amber's back. She turned and studied the man sitting at the table. Would she even know if she was staring at a killer?

"Does your mother still live at the same address?" There was a slight difference to Perry's voice. She doubted Chess picked up on it.

"No, sir. She moved two years ago." If Chess was

the Jacobstown Hacker, would he admit to knowing the area so freely? "My stepdad got work in Houston so they headed south."

"Do you come back to Jacobstown to visit friends?"

"Didn't have any. I'd stop by my mother's for lunch on Sunday a couple times a month. We didn't go out. I'd watch the game with Paul, her husband, and then head home," he admitted.

Zach's phone pinged. He checked the screen. "Coroner is sending over pictures of the victim."

Amber searched Rylan's face. He may not have had a relationship with the woman who could very well be the victim, but that didn't mean this would be easy. He'd spent time with her. They'd had a child. Granted, he didn't know about Brooklyn until two days ago, but a child connected people whether they wanted to be or not. She thought about the child she'd lost. About her ex, Red Coker. Losing their child had broken their relationship. Every time she thought about what happened to her baby, she ached. The pain hit her full force, like it had happened yesterday.

She shoved the thoughts down deep and refocused on Zach, who was pulling up an image on his phone.

He must've texted the deputy in the next room because he told Chess to sit tight and then left the room.

Chess fidgeted with his hands before leaning forward and resting his elbows on his knees. His right leg was going a mile a minute.

Zach stared at the image on his phone as he shared it with Rylan.

"There's no birthmark on her neck," Rylan pointed out. "It can't be her."

"Can I see? I might be able to help." She handed the baby to Rylan before walking over and standing next to her cousin. She wanted to protect the innocence of the child even though Brooklyn would have no idea what she was looking at. It didn't take but a second to recognize the victim. "I know who she is. That's Breanna Griswold."

Zach muttered a curse under his breath. "I remember that family."

"They moved away a few years ago saying they wanted a fresh start after Breanna got into trouble here. We were in the same grade in school, but we didn't hang out. She used to skip a lot. I think she got held back for nonattendance after freshman year of high school. I always felt so bad for her. She seemed sad all the time." Amber had invited her to sit together at lunch, but Breanna flat-out refused. "She kept to herself and never socialized. I saw her a few times hanging out with the McFarland boys, and we all know they turned out to be bad news."

Rylan suddenly got very still. She remembered overhearing a fight between him and Will about those brothers years ago. She figured this wasn't the time to reopen those old wounds. It was obvious by Will's actions earlier that he hadn't forgiven Rylan for whatever happened between them in the past.

She turned to Rylan. "Did you know her?"

He shook his head. "I have no idea why she would've been on the ranch."

Brooklyn tried to jam her entire fist inside her mouth. She started fidgeting in Rylan's arms.

"She's probably getting hungry," Amber stated, ignoring the look Zach issued. He could look all he wanted. It wouldn't stop her from getting to know Rylan's daughter. Besides, that man needed a hand if anyone did. He admittedly had no idea how to take care of a child. He didn't exactly have time to learn, either. She'd literally been thrust in his arms two days ago. "Can I help you get a bottle ready in the break room?"

Rylan glanced at Zach. "I don't want to get in the way of a family discussion."

He must've picked up on the feeling of being the monkey in the middle. She wasn't trying to put him in that position.

"Zach, you have anything else you want to say to me?" Amber's balled fist was on her hip now.

Her cousin shot a defeated look toward her. "I'm good."

"Then it's settled. I can take you to the break room. There's a microwave in there where we can heat up her bottle." Amber motioned for Rylan to follow. She thought about the offer to keep Brooklyn at the ranch and figured the idea deserved more consideration.

With a glance in Zach's direction, Rylan joined her in the hallway. He turned back to the sheriff. "Let me know if Chess says anything worth hearing."

"You bet."

"I can take her or the diaper bag. Which is a better help?" Rylan asked.

"You want to hold this muffin so I can figure out how to heat her bottle in that microwave? I never come here anymore," she admitted.

Brooklyn fussed the minute her daddy took her in his arms. "I don't think she likes me very much."

"You'll get the hang of it, Rylan. Give yourself a chance. The two of you just met." Amber looked at the baby, who was working up to belt out another cry. Her heart fisted while everything inside Amber rushed to comfort the baby. Yeah, she was in deep trouble. "I'll take her back and you can make the bottle."

"She met you *after* me." Rylan admitted defeat as he handed over the little girl. He followed Amber down the hallway and into the break room.

Amber rattled off instructions for heating the bottle as she rocked Brooklyn, offering what little comfort she could when all the baby really wanted to do was fill her belly.

Fifteen minutes and one crazy messed-up bib

later, Brooklyn was sucking on a bottle of formula. It was dangerous to get too attached, Amber thought. And then she looked into those beautiful brown eyes that looked so much like the baby's daddy.

Thoughts of Breanna struck, of her family and how they would have to hear the worst news ever. Now Breanna's parents would suffer the heartbreak no parent should ever have to endure. Granted, Amber didn't wish that particular brand of pain on anyone. Having heard rumors about the family, she knew they wouldn't be described as close-knit. Did that really matter?

To her thinking, pain was pain. Loss was loss. And she wished she'd made even more of an effort to reach out to Breanna back in school. Would it have made a difference? Amber would like to think that everyone's actions could. Was she living in a fantasy world?

Maybe she didn't want to live in a world where they didn't.

Looking at Brooklyn, at her innocence, Amber had to believe that everyone could make a difference in someone else's life. She would already do anything for the little girl in her arms. The thought was dangerous.

Could she open up her heart again?

Chapter Twelve

Rylan studied Amber as Brooklyn slept against her chest. Ellen Haiden, Zach's secretary, had dimmed the lights in the break room, and Amber had moved to a leather club couch that was backed up against the east facing wall.

"I'm sorry about your friend," Rylan said.

"That's the thing—she wasn't."

He cocked an eyebrow.

"She had trouble at home. I heard rumors that she had it pretty rough. I invited her to sit at my lunch table, but she refused. I gave up even though I knew I shouldn't have." Her voice was laced with regret.

"How old were you?"

"I was in ninth grade. Old enough to know better," she said.

"Most kids that age can't be bothered to think about anyone but themselves. The fact that you noticed says how special you are." He took a seat on the arm of the couch and touched her cheek. Outside of the break room, activity was a blur. Here, with Amber, time seemed to slow and the setting felt intimate. It was just her. Being with her stirred places inside him. He still wasn't ready to figure out what that meant, but he was intrigued. No one had ever held his attention like she did. He'd never felt a draw this strong or wanted to reach out and touch a woman this badly.

And that's where he put on the brakes.

Amber was a friend, probably his only friend. He didn't need to go messing around with that. As long as he was in Jacobstown, and for the first time in his life he was thinking about sticking around somewhere more than a minute, he needed that friend.

Part of him wanted to say that he needed her, but he shut it down before it could gain any traction. Rylan didn't *need* anyone. He did, however, appreciate her help. So he wouldn't repay her kindness by taking her to bed, even though she gave him signs and his body tried to convince him it wouldn't end in disaster.

Besides, Will hated Rylan enough already. He didn't want to hurt his former best friend any further.

When Rylan had called Amber, he thought he was asking for a favor that might last a couple of hours. He never would've signed her up for what was going on. "You sure you want to keep doing this?"

"Doing what?" She bit back a yawn.

"Stick with me. I realize you're in danger, Amber.

And you have a heart bigger than Texas, which is saying a lot. But there are places you could go to be safe," he said.

"Where? Like the ranch?" She twisted her mouth. "Look how well that worked out for Breanna."

She made a point. And he was still trying to figure out why she would've been on the family's ranch in the first place.

"Besides, Rylan, how do you know you didn't save my life?"

Now she was going overboard. "What does that mean exactly?"

"If I'd been on the ranch, that could've been me. This jerk was ready to strike. He's been ready. He's been biding his time, waiting for the right opportunity. What if that had been me out there instead of Breanna?" He couldn't argue the logic. And he appreciated her trying to take the burden off him.

"I hear what you're saying. We go back a long time," he started, "so don't take what I'm saying the wrong way. But I'd never forgive myself if anything happened to you because you were helping me."

She stared at him for a long moment. He expected her to put up a fight, but she seemed to be contemplating his words instead. She pursed full pink lips, and then she spoke. "I understand."

Silence sat between them, and he gave her a minute to rethink her position.

"I hear you, Rylan. I do. You've said it more than once. No matter how much this investigation heats up, I'm committed to helping you and this baby. You have a family, Rylan. How wonderful is that?" She put her hand up before he could comment. "Granted, I know the circumstances are not ideal. We'll find this baby's mother and figure out who she's running from. But at the end of the day you have a healthy and beautiful baby girl. That's a blessing some people never get."

Her words, her loss, was a gut punch. He must seem pretty damn selfish to her, considering she'd lost a child. He couldn't argue the point that Brooklyn was a beautiful kid. He had bigger fears about what the child's mother had gotten all of them into. From the sound of Chess's statement, Brooklyn's mother was scared half out of her mind. "We don't have any idea what's really going on. If I have a chance to protect you from it, I will."

"I know that, Rylan. I appreciate the fact that you care. Right now, you need me. You don't have the first idea how to take care of this little angel." Amber held that child tight against her chest. It was easy to see that someone would need pliers to pry Brooklyn from Amber's hands.

Rylan knew when he'd lost a battle. He wanted Amber's help, just not at the risk of losing her.

So, he conceded the argument for now and paced while he waited for word from Zach.

A half hour ticked by while they waited for Chess to work with a sketch artist.

The man was scared and, better yet, willing to cooperate. He was also the last known person to see Brooklyn's mother alive. Rylan could only hope she wasn't physically harmed. After hearing the story from Chess, it was clear that Brooklyn's mother was in serious danger.

About a year ago, Rylan remembered spending a lot of his leave time with a buddy. This was as good a time as any to make the phone call he'd been needing to make. Fishing out his cell, he told Amber about making the call and excused himself. It seemed wrong to talk about his time spent with another woman in front of her, like a betrayal.

Roger Hendricks answered on the first ring. "Rylan, man, are you in town?"

"Hey, Roger. Nah. I'm back in Jacobstown."

"Yeah? I heard you got out. Thought you might be up for a party," Roger said.

"Another time." Rylan had no plans to follow up on that. "I was hoping you could help me out, bro."

"Anything. You know I'd do anything for you, man," came Roger's response. The two had gone through basic training together before different deployments sent them to opposite ends of the world. They'd stayed in touch. Rylan had set his sight on elite forces, where Roger had served and then gotten the heck out, as he'd put it. His friend had said the only sand he wanted to see for the rest of his life was on a beach in the US. Rylan couldn't blame the man. Places like Kandahar weren't for everyone. "What's up?"

"I'm trying to locate a woman—"

"Who am I? Tinder?" Roger joked.

"Funny, bro. It's someone from last year. A friend of Sandy's." Sandy was Roger's girlfriend.

"Ah, yeah, Sandy. We had a good time together. But, man, we broke up months ago," he informed him.

"No worries, bro. What's Sandy's last name? Maybe I can find the person I'm looking for on her social media," Rylan explained. "It's important that I find her. I think she might be in some kind of trouble. I'd like to help her out."

"Good thinking. Bonds is her last name," Roger replied.

"Cool. Thanks, bro. I owe you one." Rylan didn't want to get into the whole baby business with his buddy. Not yet anyway. He was still coming to terms with the fact that he was that little girl's father.

He ended the call and located Zach in his office. The sheriff had a serious expression as he studied his computer screen.

Rylan knocked on the doorjamb.

"Sorry, I didn't see you standing there." Zach seemed caught off guard. "I have the sketch."

He motioned toward his desk and studied Rylan as he walked over and picked it up.

"I don't know." Rylan racked his brain. She seemed kind of familiar but he wasn't certain. "It's not ringing any bells."

"Sorry," Zach said. His tone said he meant it.

"I have the name of my buddy's ex-girlfriend. I just got off the phone with him a few minutes ago. I might be able to use her social media page to locate our mystery woman. Do you have a tablet I can borrow? Amber and I can search social media sites and see what we can come up with," Rylan said.

"Great idea." Zach searched around on his desk, and had to move a couple of files before he uncovered a tablet. He held it up. "Here you go."

Rylan thanked him and returned to the break room with the tablet in hand. He sat next to Amber. "Let's see what we can find on this."

"Who are we looking for?" Amber's shoulder touched his, and he ignored the impact the contact had on him. When the time was right, he planned to address it. He also planned to see how far another kiss would take them even though he knew better than to go there in his mind.

"I have the name of one of Brooklyn's mother's friends. Sandy Bonds. I thought we could check social media now that we have a face to go on."

He set the sketch of the mystery woman on his

leg while he pulled up a popular social media site on the tablet and performed a search for Sandy Bonds. Several faces popped up. He searched each one until he recognized her.

"There she is. There's Sandy Bonds." Amber studied the page.

"Who has seven hundred–plus friends?" Rylan asked under his breath. Close friends he could count on one hand. Okay, maybe his best friend was sitting next to him. And that was another reason why he shouldn't be thinking about the kiss they'd shared or wanting more than that from her.

"I never did get into social media other than for the ranch. I started our page and post every once in a while on it," Amber said. "It helped get word out when we were changing our practices in order to provide organic meats to our customers."

Rylan remembered that he'd read something about her being a pioneer in the beef industry. He admired her business savvy, but he also knew she respected her animals.

He scrolled through the faces, searching for a resemblance to the sketch. Zach strolled in and joined them, sitting on the opposite side of Amber.

And then it happened. The face he was searching for filled the screen.

"Alicia Ward." Zach said the name out loud most likely hoping to trigger a memory.

"We have a name." Rylan shrugged. "It doesn't ring any bells for me, but at least we have a face and a name to go with it. Let's figure out who she is. Click on her page."

"Mind if I?" Zach clicked on the tile with her face and a profile filled the screen. Rylan would call this progress, except there wasn't much on her page save for a few stock pictures of animals with cutesy quotes underneath.

"How much do people have to fill out in order to show up on one of these sites?" Rylan asked.

"Not much and any information can be faked," Amber said. "There aren't as many controls as you'd think there should be. Pretty much anyone can make a page as long as they don't put up strange or offensive material to get their page reported."

Zach scrolled through the animal pictures, no doubt looking for some kind of clue about the woman they searched for. "There's no information about who she is or where she's from. Do you know if she's even from Texas?"

"We met in Austin while I was stationed in San Antonio for a training exercise. I was in and out in a few weeks. Went to my friend's house a couple of times in Austin. Hit Sixth Street to listen to live music. I'd been through a stressful time overseas, and Roger thought I needed to get out more." Rylan tried to force the memory. He had a beautiful baby girl whose DNA matched his own. He ought to be able to remember the child's mother.

"Sandy should be easy enough to find. Her information is accessible." Some of Zach's confidence had returned. "You said Alicia is Sandy's friend."

"That's right." All Rylan could remember from those few times in Austin was hanging around with Roger. Most of the weekends were clear as a bell. There was one he couldn't make heads or tails out of, and that bugged him to no end. Guilt and a strong sense of shame slammed into him. Rylan had never considered himself weak, so a binge weekend seemed impossible. And yet the evidence sat in Amber's arms.

He fished out his cell and called Roger back. "Hey, sorry to bother you again. Do you mind if I ask a strange question?"

"Not at all, man. Go for it," Roger said.

"Was I sober when we hung out?" The question probably seemed out of the blue.

"You don't remember?" Based on the surprise in Roger's voice, Rylan had caught his friend off guard.

"I know I didn't choose to drink. But that's not the same thing as being sober—"

"Well, I didn't force anything down your throat," Roger joked.

Rylan let the conversation stay lighthearted. It was embarrassing to have to ask. He didn't remember falling off the wagon so why was that one weekend so fuzzy? Why didn't he remember the mother of his child or the making of his child? Hell, he should remember that, at least.

"Let me think back. Damn, it's been a while since we hung out, and you were definitely a saint. No drinking. But, yeah, there was that one time I wondered about you." His friend got quiet.

"What did I do?"

"Slurred your speech. You sounded...I don't know...*off*. Not like yourself. I even asked what you were drinking, but you denied having a beer." Roger paused. "Which was strange because I'm not the saint you think I am. I remember thinking there was no reason to lie to me."

"Was I with a woman that night? Do you remember me being with someone?" Rylan moved his lips away from the mouthpiece and focused on Zach. "Can you send that picture over to him?"

Zach nodded. He got Roger's number from Rylan and texted Alicia's photo.

A minute passed before Roger responded. "Wow, yeah, I remember this woman. What did you say her name was again?"

"Alicia Ward," Rylan said.

Roger drew in a breath. "Of course I remember her. A person remembers someone as good-looking as her. Especially when she comes on to his buddy. I was with Sandy then so it didn't bother me. But she was smokin' hot and seemed pretty locked on to you. You didn't stay in touch?"

"No. I don't remember much about her, and that's throwing me off because I quit drinking and got my act together when I signed up for the military." Rylan wasn't frustrated with his friend. He was frustrated with himself. "I don't remember drinking that night because I don't drink anymore."

"If a woman who looked like that came on to me, I'd remember." Roger's comment issued a strong response from Amber.

She grunted and Zach turned his head to face her. He seemed to know better than to say anything once he got a good look at her expression.

Hell, Rylan knew better than to poke the bear. Part of him—a part he shouldn't give much credence to— liked the fact that Amber seemed jealous. He knew better than to let the thought take seed. "I don't remember much about that weekend, to be honest. Do you remember if I did anything to embarrass myself in public?"

"I had my own thing going, and it's been a long time. Nothing that stands out," Roger said.

It was too soon to be relieved and Rylan wasn't any closer to answers, but if he'd slipped he was fairly certain Roger would've known it. Which didn't explain why he didn't remember Alicia. All he remembered drinking that night was soda.

"Thanks, bro. If you remember anything, will you give me a shout?" It was worth asking even though Rylan doubted anything would spark. A year was a long time to recall something that happened over a weekend. And to a buddy.

"Will do, man."

Rylan ended the call after saying goodbye.

"I'll be able to dig around now that we have a name. I'll get my secretary on a hunt for Brooklyn's birth certificate. That woman works miracles when it comes to research. Now that we know you're the father and we have a mother's name, there are two possibilities for last names, which will narrow the field." Zach's mind was clicking through his next steps. Those seemed like good places to start.

"I keep wondering why the unmarked car from earlier sat behind us for so long without making a move. When we bolted, he didn't try to shoot, either." That was just two of the puzzle pieces not clicking in Rylan's mind. "I keep coming back to the fact they were casing us." He turned to Zach. "There another reason you can think of?"

"I agree with you. They most likely wanted to see who is involved and monitor the threat level for when they come back," Zach stated.

"Why keep coming back at all?" Amber had been

quiet for the past few minutes, and Rylan didn't necessarily see that as a positive sign.

"It's obvious that someone wants Brooklyn." Zach rubbed the scruff on his chin. "You want my honest opinion?"

Amber shot a look that dared him to go ahead.

"The mother got herself in some kind of trouble or decided to sell her baby to a ruthless baby ring. There's big money in black-market adoptions. A couple might have been promised this child and then the mother reneged. Maybe she didn't want to go along with this in the first place but felt she had no choice. So, she figures out another way, panics at the last minute and then backs out of the agreement. These guys aren't having any of that, so they come after the girl. Only these guys don't ask permission. They're used to taking what they want. They get things done. I'll send a deputy out to speak to Sandy Bonds and see if we can get any information about her friend. This could take a few days, so I want both of you to be prepared for that. I need a little time to investigate, and I need to know all three of you will be safe in the meantime. You're welcome to stay at my house."

Brooklyn woke up and started fussing, interrupting Zach. From what Rylan gathered so far about babies, she would need a bottle and a diaper change. "We appreciate the offer, Zach, but we'll figure out a good spot."

"How could anyone abandon a sweet little baby like this?" Amber's eyes sparked as she repositioned Brooklyn onto the couch beside her in order to change the little one's diaper. "Trouble or not, what kind of person could just drop her off with a stranger and run? She had no idea this man would come find you. He could've done anything he wanted to this little girl."

What did that say? Rylan let the thought sit for a few minutes. He liked to think of himself as a good judge of character. Going on a bender and having a baby with a near-stranger weren't shining examples of good behavior. Those weren't making the high-light reel of his life.

Again, he thought about the drinking and chided himself. How could he have allowed this to happen? He'd been to parties with beautiful women before and had never gotten out of control. The urge to drink never went away, but as the years went by sobriety got easier to maintain. He couldn't remember the last time he'd been tempted.

"If you two will excuse me, I have some work I need to get back to. I'll return as soon as I have something more to talk about." He extended his hand and Rylan shook it. "I said it before but welcome back to town."

Chapter Thirteen

"A sheriff's office is no place for a baby." Amber hugged the little girl tighter to her chest. She'd changed and helped feed Brooklyn, but the baby had a hard time settling back down. "She's probably just picking up on all this energy. We're too stressed, and she's reading us and there's too much activity for her to go to sleep."

"Can babies do that?" Rylan paced circles around the break room while gently bouncing Brooklyn. Seeing such a strong man being so gentle with a little one cracked a little more of the casing around Amber's meticulously guarded heart.

"Pick up on energy?" She looked at him. "I believe so. I've seen it with my nieces and nephews. If not that, she could have a fever."

Rylan stopped long enough for her to touch the baby's forehead.

"Is she hot?"

"No. Not that I want her to be sick, but that would

explain why she's so fussy." Amber followed as Rylan made another lap.

"Everything she's known for the past three months has changed. She might just be reacting to wanting her mother." He made a good point.

"I can't imagine what would have to happen for me to be willing to be away from my child." Amber's cheeks almost caught fire for how much she burned on the inside thinking about Brooklyn's circumstances.

"I don't remember her." Rylan stopped. "How much of a jerk does that make me?"

"It's weird. Don't you think? You don't remember drinking and, Rylan, I believe you. You vaguely remember spending time with someone, but it's all hazy. Have you thought about the fact that this woman might've slipped something in your—" she paused for a second "—Coke or tea or whatever you were drinking?"

"Coffee."

"At a party?" Amber wasn't a drinker but even she didn't drink coffee at night. And she loved her some coffee.

"It was winter. Cold outside and I'm not much on soda." His honesty shouldn't make her want to laugh. There was something pure in those words and she was more convinced than ever that he didn't drink, even though she couldn't prove it and all evidence pointed to him doing just that. "I'd just gotten back from a deployment and was undergoing some training in San Antonio. I had leave so I called Roger. I wanted to get the hell off base and away from anyone wearing combat boots."

Was he talking about something real with her? Not just cracking a joke when a subject got too intense like when they were kids? She liked the fact that he'd opened up to her. She could see the pain in his features when he talked about the possibility of him drinking.

"Did something happen overseas?" She wondered if that was part of the reason he'd doubted himself.

"A lot happened over there, most of which I can't talk about. But the worst of it, the worst of human kind came when a grandmother strapped an IUD to her grandson and sent him toward a bunch of us." He stopped like he needed a minute. Brooklyn fussed a little more, and he picked up where he left off pacing.

"That must've been horrific to watch." Again, she couldn't fathom a parent or grandparent who could do something so awful.

"The kid didn't make it near any of us. His life was sacrificed for nothing. Don't get me wrong, I didn't want any of my fellow SEALs to die—"

"I get it. You wanted his life to mean something. He was young, innocent. If he had to die, it should be for something," she said.

He stopped and locked eyes with her for a long moment. It was like time froze and the earth shifted. Sure, he was handsome and she'd been attracted to him from the time they were in high school. This grown-up crush just got real. And she couldn't allow the seed that had been planted to grow because her heart ached for Rylan.

So she cleared her throat and refocused on Brooklyn.

"She probably just needs to get out of here. Your arms must be breaking by now. Do you want me to take a turn with her?" She diverted her gaze because she didn't want to look him in the eyes when she felt so vulnerable.

"I got this. Looks like I'll have to get used to it just being me and her at some point. I appreciate all your help, but I have to learn how to care for my daughter."

"Rylan, do you want to hear a shock?"

He nodded.

"You're going to be an amazing dad."

"I doubt that. But I plan to give it my all. My failures won't be from lack of trying, that's for damn sure." He patted Brooklyn's back, but she only fussed more.

"Maybe try sitting down with her." She glanced at the wall clock. "It's time for another bottle."

It was getting late. They'd been at the sheriff's office for at least twelve hours. They both knew they needed to leave at some point. They couldn't stay there all night, not with a baby who needed some comforts.

Amber made a bottle. She needed something to do with her hands anyway.

Rylan settled onto the sofa with the little girl in his arms. He carefully positioned her so he could free his right hand in order to feed her the bottle. She settled down almost immediately as she latched on to the plastic nipple. He had that satisfied smile that dented his cheek. Her heart stirred even though she ordered it to behave.

That was the thing about being with Rylan. Her emotions were as out of control as he was. Amber wouldn't change a thing about him, either.

"It might be easier to transport her once she's sleeping. We'll have a few hours to make our move before she'll need tending to again," Rylan said, his voice a low rumble.

"Where should we go and how should we get there?" Amber asked as Zach walked into the room.

"I got a hit on the birth certificate. The baby's name is Brooklyn Ward, and she was born in a hospital in San Marcos," Zach informed them. "Her mother listed her occupation as a homemaker. She didn't list a father's name."

"That's not surprising given the circumstances," Rylan said.

"The hospital where she gave birth has a reputation for covering up illegal adoptions," Zach warned. "It seems we were on track with the adoption ring."

"Can a baby be adopted without the father's consent?" Rylan made a good point. Amber didn't have a lot of knowledge of the adoption process, but the question was reasonable.

"In the state of Texas, when there's no father on record or at the birth, judges usually side with the mother," Zach informed him.

"How can we find out if paperwork was filed? Or if an adoption has been started?" Rylan started firing questions.

"She can't be taken away from you legally now that paternity is being established. Technically it already has been, but I'm talking about in the eyes of the law. My favorite lab should be able to confirm what we already know. Brooklyn is your daughter." Zach glanced from Rylan to Amber. "Why do I get the feeling the two of you were about to leave?"

"This place isn't good for a baby. She needs a bath and clean clothes," Amber stated.

"Were you thinking of taking her back to the ranch?" Zach asked.

"That's probably not a good idea. There will be a lot of attention as soon as news of Breanna's murder gets out," Amber replied. "This office will also be inundated. How will we be able to keep this little girl protected with people coming in and out? You know as well as I do the town has been uneasy. Everyone's been fearing what just happened on the ranch, and we have no idea how much pandemonium the news will stir up."

"You're right. We're already starting to get calls. Word will spread like wildfire from here," Zach admitted.

"Where is it safe for us to go?" Amber was thinking out loud.

"Maybe it's best if we don't say. I know a place we should be safe." Rylan sounded confident, and Amber wished she shared the feeling.

As it was, she felt like she was damned if she did and damned if she didn't. Tell Zach where they were planning to hide out and their location could end up compromised. Don't tell him and there'd be no extra patrol to count on.

Deputy Perry peeked his head into the break room. "Sir, there's a couple here that has requested to speak with you."

"Can it wait? I'm in the middle of something here," Zach said.

"This couple says they're Brooklyn Ward's parents."

"THAT'S IMPOSSIBLE," AMBER said under her breath. She was on her feet in two seconds flat. "Zach—"

"I know," he reassured her. "Give me a minute

to get them inside the interview room, and then I'll send for you. Wait here."

Willpower was in short supply when it came to waiting to see who claimed to be Brooklyn's parents. The expression on Rylan's face, the steel resolve in the face of the unknown made her wish for half his strength. This couldn't be easy on him.

Zach left the room, and she wheeled around to Rylan.

"Let's just hear them out. They can't be talking about her." She offered reassurance from a shaky voice.

"She's my daughter. They'll take her away over my dead body," was all he said, but those words were loaded with the kind of truth that took on a physical manifestation. There was no room for doubt.

Deputy Perry appeared in the doorway, signaling Amber and Rylan to follow him down the familiar hallway and into the room they'd been in not that long ago. The baby had fussed herself to sleep and was cuddled against her father's shoulder.

After depositing them inside the viewing room, Deputy Perry leaned into the interview room and gave a thumbs-up.

"Please state your name for the record." Zach's posture was relaxed as he leaned over a pad of paper that was sitting atop the table and looked at the male sitting across from him.

There were three people present. A couple who looked to be in their late forties or early fifties and a man wearing one of those crisp expensive buttoned-up collars tucked inside an even more expensive navy blue business suit. The man in the navy suit sat ramrod straight and had an intensity about him, like if he ordered a hamburger at a fast-food restaurant people would immediately get nervous about making it perfect.

The couple also wore suits, cut from material that would classify them as power suits. From what Amber could tell, there was a lot of money sitting across that table. She figured it was old money because everything the couple wore was understated, expensive and classic. There was nothing showy like people with new money gravitated toward.

Wealthy ranchers were a different breed. She noticed the differences all too well growing up. Her father would welcome anyone to the dinner table who was honest and worked hard. Ranch hands often got invited to her mother's legendary Sunday suppers, with food that Amber still could almost taste when she thought hard enough, and missed to this day.

Amber gravitated toward salt-of-the-earth types. If she and Rylan didn't have such a long history, he'd be the kind of man she'd want to date. But then, men she actually wanted to go out with had been in short supply in the past couple of years. Add to the fact that Amber worked fourteen-hour days and she had no time for socializing. It was fine with her except that she could admit to feeling like her life was missing something lately.

She chalked up her change of heart to all the happiness around her. Amy had found happiness with Isaac. Zach recently reconnected with the love of his life.

"My clients' names are Veronica and Cornell Robinson. They received information that their adopted daughter is here in your office." The Suit bent to his right and pulled a manila file folder out of his black briefcase. He set the file on the table between him and used two fingers from each hand to push the file toward Zach.

"What's the basis for Mr. and Mrs. Robinson's claim?" Zach ignored the manila file, and that seemed to irk the Suit.

Amber had seen her cousin at work and in action many times before, and all she could say was the man had found his calling. He had a way of cutting through the layers and getting down to what was really important. He had a way with people and could get them to talk. Being sheriff suited him to perfection.

"Open the folder and you'll see for yourself." The Suit leaned back in his chair, folded his arms and crossed his legs.

"Whatever's in there won't hold up in court," Zach informed him, and Mrs. Robinson issued an over-the-top grunt. It was her turn to act indignant.

"We can do this the hard way, but I can see that you're a busy man and there's no reason to waste anyone's time." The Suit didn't realize he was already outplayed. At this point, this matchup was like watching a Little League team versus the Texas Rangers.

Amber could only see the back of Zach's head, and she wished for a better view of his face. It was his turn to lean back in his chair like he was in a hammock in the Caribbean. She could almost see his expression, having witnessed it so many times when he was on the verge of winning an argument. And growing up with five brothers and a male cousin who'd spent half his childhood at the ranch, she knew a thing or two about when someone was defeated.

"Do they look familiar to you?" Amber asked Rylan.

"I've never seen these people in my life." He seemed to be going to great lengths to keep a cool head, and she appreciated the fact that he'd taken her seriously about the baby picking up on emotions.

"Strange," she whispered. "The guys in the sedan and pickup from earlier might've been able to take her if they'd really wanted to, but they didn't. They let us go. Granted, you drove the heck out of my SUV in order to get around that sedan, but they let us go."

"I figured they were casing it and planning to

come back in with muscle. I never saw this coming," Rylan admitted. "They didn't want to risk her being hurt because these guys want her in one piece is my best guess."

"My clients demand to take their daughter home, and if you would open that file, you'd see they're within their rights to do so and this mix-up can be resolved."

Mrs. Robinson wore her suit and pearls to perfection. Her hair was cut in a bob that flattered her oval-shaped face. She wore enough makeup to cover any blemishes on her face. It was almost too perfect. When Amber really looked at the woman, she noticed that she had on a considerable amount of foundation. What was she covering? Was she sick? Was Mr. Robinson physically abusive?

This couple looked like they could legitimately adopt a child. Based on appearances, money didn't seem to be a problem. So, if they'd used a sketchy adoption agency, there had to be something lurking in their background. Amber agreed with Rylan. Brooklyn would leave this office with them over her dead body, as well.

Zach extended his hand to the lawyer. "Forgive my manners. My name is Zach McWilliams."

The Suit obliged.

"What makes you so sure I have a baby here in my office?" Zach asked.

The attorney leveled his gaze. "Are you denying it?"

Amber rolled her eyes. It was just like a fancy overdressed lawyer to dodge the question. "Zach has a good point. How do they know the baby they claim belongs to them is here?"

"Brooklyn Ward's birth mother, Alicia Ward, signed over parental rights to my clients," the Suit said.

"Sorry, I didn't catch your name." Zach picked up the pen in front of him and leaned forward again, ready to write.

"Teague Thompson." The man was playing it too cool. He was either as big of a deal as he would have Zach believe, or he was big-time bluffing.

Zach made a show of looking at his cell phone. Then came, "Will you folks excuse me?"

Teague Thompson pursed his lips and studied Zach before finally nodding.

Mrs. Robinson made a dramatic show of throwing her arms in the air.

"Do you see any real tears?" Rylan asked as he studied the woman's face through the mirror.

"Nope. Not one. I doubt she'd smudge her makeup with any," Amber said in a low voice.

Zach stopped in the hallway outside the opened door. The lights were dimmed inside the room, and it gave an almost intimate feeling.

Amber knew how this worked. As long as it was

dark in the room, she was in the clear. The occupants of the adjacent room were none the wiser about who watched. By contrast, the interview room's lights were bright fluorescents.

Zach waved them into the hallway. Deputy Perry stood watch over the interview room door, arms folded against his chest and with his back to the door. He looked like a bull waiting to be baited, and it was obvious that wouldn't go well for the challenger. Amber knew from experience not to mess with a determined deputy. Her cousin hired only the best of the best, and the most loyal. He'd said that he could train someone how to do the job, but he couldn't train personality, work ethic or loyalty.

"This is an unexpected development." Zach raked his fingers through his hair.

"What's your take on the husband and wife?" Amber wondered if he picked up on the signs she saw.

"She's either sick or being abused." He didn't hesitate with his opinion, and it confirmed what she'd already been thinking.

"My thoughts exactly." Amber trusted her instincts but confirmation from Zach left no room for doubt. If Mr. Robinson had a history of abuse, no legitimate adoption agency in Texas would give the couple a baby.

"I can run a background check on him because they have a connection to Brooklyn's mother, who has gone missing. I can threaten to hold them both and interview them all I want. They've already lawyered up, and my experience tells me that they've been coached on how to answer any question I might bring up." Zach made good points. Even though she and Rylan were on the right side of the law, a good attorney knew how to manipulate the truth and find loopholes.

"Think we should stick around?" Rylan asked her.

Of course, in her mind the law always won out, but that was probably fairy-tale thinking mixed with good intentions.

"If you're not here, they can't accidentally see her. I can't lie to them, but I'm not obligated to volunteer information, either." Zach's face was a study in determination.

"I'd like to hear what they have to say. Why they think they have a claim to her," Amber interjected.

"Then stick around. Just know that they most likely will recognize the baby, and it could get messy," he informed her.

Brooklyn stirred and Amber's heart went into free fall. The last thing the little girl needed was to hear shouting or conflict. Zach was right. Even though she'd settled down for the moment, it was only a matter of time before she'd wake again and start fussing.

"What are the chances their claim is legitimate?" Rylan's jaw clenched, and she could see the question wasn't easy for him to ask.

Chapter Fourteen

"If all the players are on the court, I'd say we have the upper hand right now. I've learned not to take anything for granted when it comes to the law. I don't know who these folks might be connected to because I get the impression they're important. If they support someone in a higher office, I could get a phone call. My hands could be tied and that's not a feeling I like. A skilled lawyer could tie up the case for months, possibly years. And even if we get justice at some point, these two could relocate to Europe or Mexico and take Brooklyn with them." Zach spoke the truth and even though it wasn't what Rylan necessarily wanted to hear, he needed to consider every word carefully.

No one was prying Brooklyn out of his hands now that he knew she was his daughter.

"I wanted to give you a heads-up. I'm going back in that room, and at some point during the interview I'll be forced to open the file and see what evidence they think they've presented. If they know she's here, it'll make it more difficult for me to deny that I know her whereabouts. But something's brewing for them to come down here like this and demand custody. I took an oath to uphold the law. My instincts have to take second place."

Rylan figured as much. "What are you planning to tell them?"

"That this is my jurisdiction and every citizen, including the ones not old enough to defend themselves, deserve my protection. Here's the thing. I don't technically have proof that you're Brooklyn's father, and I might get caught in a legal loophole." He scratched his chin. "They might be bluffing, but I don't know what cards they have up their sleeves. Showing up here and boldly demanding custody of Brooklyn leads me to believe they haven't shown all of their hand yet."

Rylan nodded his understanding.

"I better get back inside. Think about what I said," Zach said.

Rylan thanked him and fisted his hands. The sedan and pickup could be outside waiting for them in case they made a run for it. He thought about their dwindling options. He and Amber couldn't take the baby back to his place. They couldn't take her to the ranch, either. There were too many witnesses, and Rylan would never ask another Kent to cover for him.

Amber urged him back into the small viewing room and closed the door.

"We have the right to demand to see our daughter." Mr. Robinson had the authoritative voice of someone used to being in charge at home and at the office. If Rylan had to guess, he'd figure the man for someone who ran his own business and not an abuse victim.

"How old is your daughter?" Zach asked.

"Three months and two days," Mrs. Robinson piped up. Amber was right; there was something off about the woman that didn't sit right with him. The thought that the man seemed to be abusive with his wife sat like a nail in Rylan's stomach. Mrs. Robinson could best be described as…broken. She forced her shoulders straight, but Rylan could see that she wasn't used to being assertive. To make matters worse, Mr. Robinson's posture was tense, aggressive.

"When was the last time you saw the baby's mother?" Zach looked up from his notepad.

"No one said my clients have met the mother," the lawyer interjected.

Mrs. Robinson shot a nervous glance toward her husband, who held a solid glare aimed at Zach.

Mr. Thompson took Mrs. Robinson's hands in his. She bowed her head in dramatic fashion, and her shoulders rocked as though she was sobbing. She put on a good show.

"My clients were supposed to be given access to their daughter three days ago. The birth mother failed to show." It was the lawyer's turn to glare at Zach. "If you'd open the file, you could read all this in the report. As you can see, my client is distraught. We'd like to wrap this up and go home."

Wrap it up?

Rylan's daughter wasn't a present. He didn't like much about the adoptive parents and wondered if Alicia had gotten cold feet once she met them. It wouldn't do a lot of good to speculate, considering they were light on details. But his gut burned with fury.

"What kind of vehicle do you drive?" Zach asked.

"Excuse me?" The question seemed to catch Teague off guard. "What myself or my clients drive is not relevant to this discussion."

"It is to me." Zach paused while Mrs. Robinson pulled out a packet of tissues from a designer-looking handbag. "What's the harm in telling me?"

"My clients don't have to explain what kind of car they drive or what they're doing in town. Their daughter is here—"

"How exactly do you know that?" Zach opened the file and looked at the first piece of paper. "It says here that you're from Fort Worth. Arlington Heights. How do you know what's going on here in my town if you live an hour and forty-five minutes away?"

Rylan knew enough about the city to realize that

was an expensive neighborhood. That part didn't surprise him. He, like Zach, was curious how they'd tracked Brooklyn to Jacobstown if they weren't working with the drivers of the black sedan and pickup truck from earlier.

"Fine. We'd hoped that it wouldn't come to this, but we'd like to report a kidnapping." The lawyer had that card ready to play quickly. He'd anticipated some of Zach's moves. With an expensive suit like the one he was wearing, he looked prepared to earn his keep.

"I'm not admitting that the child is even in my county. However, if this alleged child is here in Jacobstown, you need to be very clear on one thing. She won't be leaving without a court order and/or DNA test—"

"My clients have rights, Sheriff. If you look at the second piece of paper in that folder, you'll see that a judge agrees." Teague looked a little too smug.

"And I have a right to investigate a missing person—"

"This is a kidnapping case—"

"I'm talking about Alicia Ward, the birth mother. My guess is that you already know she's disappeared. What I'm unclear on is why you believe her child is in my county." Zach slapped the folder closed and shoved it toward Teague.

Rylan turned to Amber. "Let's get her out of here."

"Okay. But where will we go?" she asked.

"Maybe it's best if we don't say. I know a place we should be safe." Rylan sounded confident and Amber wished she shared the feeling.

"THOSE PEOPLE COULD'VE ended up raising your daughter and you never would've known any different." Amber had been holding her thoughts in too long. She had no idea what kind of person Alicia Ward was, but the woman must've had some heart to back out of the deal at the last minute. "I have so many questions, Rylan."

"Like?" He got behind the wheel after she'd secured Brooklyn, and he'd made sure no one seemed too interested in what they were doing. It was past nine in the evening and they'd been at her cousin's office for thirteen hours. Her back was stiff and she was tired of sitting.

"If Alicia had known she was going to adopt out her baby, why wait three months? Why take care of her that long and then dump her on a family? Of course, the other question is why change her mind and have her brought to you? Was her pregnancy a scam? She gets herself pregnant and sells the baby but has been on the run for three months because she changes her mind and decides to keep the baby? And then she realizes that someone is after her or someone was getting close and so she tries to get the baby to you, who, by the way, has no idea she's coming or that he's even a father."

"All good points." He paused for a minute as he navigated out of the parking lot and onto the narrow street. "I still don't remember her or much about that weekend."

"And don't you think that's odd?"

"Look, I made a mistake. I must've fallen off the wagon—"

"What if you didn't, Rylan?"

"I'm not ready to let myself off the hook. It's happened before," he admitted.

"Years ago you slipped. But you said yourself that this time was different." Amber wasn't letting him hang guilt around his shoulders like that. Not if he was innocent.

"That doesn't mean anything—"

"You've been beating yourself up over this, Rylan. And if you did it, then that's fine. But—"

"No 'but.' I can't make excuses for myself, Amber. Don't you see that? It's too easy for a person like me to slip and fall down that slope again. I'd been under a lot of stress. I might've picked up a beer."

"You just don't remember it," she countered.

"That doesn't mean I didn't do it, dammit." Frustration poured off him in waves. Guilt and shame seemed to clock him.

"I believe in you," she said calmly.

"Well, don't."

She let that sit between them for a few minutes.

"Can you answer a question?" she asked.

"I can try."

"Those couple of other times that you said you fell off the wagon early on. Do you remember the first drink?" Amber gripped her cell.

"Yeah. I do. Clearly."

"But not *this* time," she continued.

"What, are you a prosecutor now? I already said that I don't remember any of it." His grip on the steering wheel tightened until his knuckles were white. "Are you satisfied?"

"Yes. I am." Amber gave it a moment to sink in.

"I hear what you're saying. It was different that time and that could've been because I didn't willingly take that first drink. It's a nice assumption, and one I want to be true with everything inside me. But I had a drinking problem at one time, and that means I can't make excuses. I have to take responsibility for my actions. Period. Until I know for certain that I didn't willingly take that first drink, I have no intention of cutting myself any slack."

The casual tone she was so used to in conversation with Rylan was gone. He usually covered what was going on inside with a wink and a smile. His charm was so good at seducing women, at making her fall a little bit harder for him. But this genuine side to him

was an express train to hurt. Because she was falling for him hard. "I believe in you, Rylan. I believe
that you've changed. And I believe that you're sober.
I understand what you're saying, and I appreciate
your perspective. I can only imagine how difficult
it must be for you to think you might've jeopardized
your sobriety. All I want you to do is open up to the
possibility that it wasn't your fault. We have no idea
what Alicia's intentions were. She might've signed
up to get pregnant—"

"Why would anyone do that?" Rylan cut her off.

"We don't know her circumstances. Let Zach investigate. You know he's good at his job. He'll un-
cover the truth," she said, trying to soothe him. His
commitment to his daughter only served to draw
Amber toward him even more. When she'd given
Red the unexpected pregnancy news, he'd come off
as supportive in the early days. It didn't take long for
his true feelings to surface. Red didn't want a child.
Of course, she'd learned that after the wedding. At
eighteen, she'd been young and naive. Had she been
in love with Red? No. She cared about him, though.
And she'd believed a relationship could grow from
there. That they could grow to love each other after
becoming a family. And then their child had been
stillborn. Red had packed his bags and moved out
before she made it home from the hospital. Looking
back, he'd done them both a favor because being a

Kent would've caused her to stick out their relationship. Kents didn't quit.

The divorce papers showed up a month later. Red had moved to California and moved on with his life. It should've hurt, but instead she felt relieved that he was gone. Ever since, she could admit that she never allowed herself to get close to anyone.

Speaking of family, there was something she needed to know before she made the argument that they might be safer at the ranch, just not at the main house. "Rylan, what happened between you and my brother?"

"It's between me and your brother." Rylan's tone had a definiteness to it that she ignored.

"I need to know."

"Why? What purpose could it possibly serve?" He white-knuckled the steering wheel.

"I changed my mind. I think we should go to the ranch for a few—"

"Forget it." Those two words had the sharpness of a blade and the finality of death.

"There's security at the main house. I know what happened to Breanna, and I reacted to that earlier but that was on the property, which we both know is vast," she argued.

"I still don't like the idea," he admitted.

"We can't just drive around all night. Being on the road isn't safe if those henchmen decide to come

back and forcibly remove Brooklyn from our arms."
Amber had no intentions of giving up easily.

"You said yourself there are flaws in ranch security." He could be a mule when he wanted to be.

Amber bit back a yawn. "There are baby supplies there. How are we supposed to take care of a three-month-old while being chased by these idiots?"

"We'll figure it out." Rylan checked the rearview mirror again, reminding her of just how much danger they were in.

"How?"

"You underestimate my abilities," he scoffed, and seemed genuinely put off by her lack of confidence in his skills as a soldier.

"I've seen how you handle yourself. Believe me when I say that if this was a one-on-one situation I'd have no doubts. But you have two handicaps, me and a baby who needs to eat every few hours and has to be handled with care. She could cry at the wrong moment, and you might not be able to cover in time. I'm not much use while I'm trying to hold her. You know that normally I know my way around a shotgun and I'm not afraid to use one. This is different, Rylan. Even a tough guy like you can see that we'll hold you back and quite possibly cost us everything. I know you're strong physically and mentally."

He grunted at that last word.

"You are, Rylan."

"We need to find Alicia Ward, and we can't do that from the ranch," he argued.

"That's a good point. We can't find her and offer the best protection for Brooklyn. If the Robinsons or their henchmen catch up to us, we might be forced to hand over your daughter and let the courts decide. You heard Zach. That could take months or years. Our family attorney would tell you the same thing if we called him." She gave him a few minutes to let those words sink in.

He concentrated harder on the stretch of road in front of them. She was getting through, making progress.

"The ranch is the safest option for Brooklyn," she added.

"That's playing dirty," he finally said.

"Maybe, but I'll do anything to keep that little angel safe and so will you. The Robinsons are going to leave Zach's office without their baby. They believe, right or wrong, that they have rights to her. Until your official DNA test comes back and proves to the courts that you're the father, we don't have any aces in our hands. Can you live with yourself if someone takes her? We only assume the vehicles were linked to the Robinsons. What if they weren't? Brooklyn could be sold off into some baby ring and literally disappear from our lives forever before we have a chance to find her." Amber risked a glance at Rylan, and she could see that her filibuster was working.

So, she stopped in order to let her argument sink in.

After circling a block three times, Rylan turned east, the direction of the ranch.

"I don't like the idea of putting your family in harm's way," he said.

"Breanna Griswold might argue that you can't protect everyone." Amber's heart fisted thinking about Breanna, about her family, about her lost life even before her death. "We need to get some rest and give Brooklyn a break. I can get enough supplies from the main house to get us through the night without alerting anyone to our presence."

"Where do you expect us to sleep without someone realizing we're there?" he asked.

"The bunkhouse." She could've sworn she saw him tense at the idea of going to the last place they'd been alone together before he left eight years ago.

Chapter Fifteen

The rest of the ride to the ranch was silent. All the
noise was going off inside Rylan's head. Thoughts
battled for attention. Frustration nailed his gut. And
he'd be damned if he wasn't thinking about the kiss
he'd shared with Amber that had been so much better than the one in the bunkhouse. There'd been so
much promise and intensity and chemistry in that
kiss. Rylan could honestly say there'd never been a
kiss like it. He wondered if that was what it was like
to have something more than a physical attraction
to someone. Although he had that, too. In spades.

He had to remind himself that he was falling down
another slippery slope and as silly as it sounded, even
to him considering he was a grown man, the promise he'd made to Will at eighteen still mattered. The
fight the two had had and the position Rylan had put
Will in still mattered. Even more so now that Rylan
was a man.

But this wasn't the time to dwell on an inappropriate attraction to his former best friend's baby sister. He almost laughed out loud at the *baby* part. Amber Kent was all woman. She helped expand the successful family cattle ranch into the powerhouse it was today and had yet to hit thirty years old. She was a force to be reckoned with. She had a sharp wit, an easy laugh and a heart that knew no bounds. And even though she'd closed off parts of herself, which he assumed had to do with the baby she'd lost, she was still the most open woman he'd ever met. One look into those eyes and he could see right through her.

Rylan refocused his attention. Dwelling on Amber's good points wasn't doing anything to quell his attraction to her—an attraction he needed to keep in check.

His thoughts were weighted with other issues. He wondered if there was a court in Texas that would take his daughter away from him. He didn't remember the girl's mother. How would that make him sound? His playboy ways might catch up to him, and Brooklyn could pay the price.

But then, if the adoption wasn't on the up-and-up, would the Robinsons want to bring this to court? Was that why they'd brought the big guns now? They'd walked into that interview room like they owned the place. When he really thought about it, Teague Thompson had played the confidence card. Mr. Robinson had seemed angry and put out. Those were understandable emotions given the fact that they'd been promised a baby who'd then disappeared. Mrs. Robinson seemed troubled. Rylan got a bad feeling every time he thought about her. And Zach had made a good point about the family's possible political connections.

"I know a private investigator who might be able to help us dig into the Robinsons' background," Amber said as they approached the gate to the ranch. "That way we won't feel like we're wasting time resting."

"That's a good idea." Rylan stopped at the guard shack.

Isaac Vanguard stood six feet one inch. He worked security at the ranch. With short, light brown hair and powder blue eyes, he would likely be considered attractive by most women.

Isaac stepped out of the building. He bent down as Rylan opened the window.

"Amy's worried about you," he said to Amber. "Said you two were supposed to be planning a lunch to benefit a women's shelter, but she hasn't been able to reach you."

Amber leaned toward the driver's side and filled Rylan's senses with her flowery and clean scent. Had she always smelled this good? "I'm sorry. I totally forgot. My cell battery died, and I keep forgetting to charge it. If you see her before I get a good charge, would you mind telling her I'll be in touch as soon as I can?"

Isaac glanced in the back seat. "Will do, ma'am."

He moved back inside the shack and pressed the button to open the gate. There was another security guard in the background, a man Rylan recognized from the other day. It seemed the Kent family was serious about adding extra security, and he saw that as a good sign they could handle almost anything that came their way. "Who was the other guy?"

"That's Blaise Dillinger." Amber rubbed her temples.

"You okay?" Rylan picked up on the tension. Granted, what they'd been through would have anyone stressed. Adrenaline had long faded from their encounter with the pickup truck and sedan, and the surprise of the Robinsons showing up at Zach's office.

"I was just turning over ideas in my head, spinning out. What if my cousin has to follow through with an investigation? The Robinsons could get a search warrant and surprise us. My family would never give us up, but they'd also be put in a bad position if they knew we were here. They'll protect us no matter the cost. They won't hesitate to stand up for us, and that could cost them if they're found in contempt of court."

"We're here. What now?" Rylan figured they were already well in over their heads.

"Would you mind doubling back to Isaac for a second?"

Rylan put the gearshift in reverse and navigated backward toward the iron gate.

Isaac must've realized something was up because he hopped out of the guard shack and jogged toward them.

"Need something?" he asked.

"If anyone asks who's at the ranch, you don't have to answer—"

"Yes, ma'am. I know." He nodded.

"I would never put you in a position to lie, Isaac—"

"I took an oath to protect this family. I've been advised of my legal rights and am aware my actions could be contested in court." Isaac's dedication was noble. "I don't have to answer any questions I don't want to. Ever. Unless I'm in a court of law being asked by a judge. It's my decision whether or not I want to put myself in jeopardy with the system. And in case you're wondering what that means, my loyalty lies with this family."

"I'm not asking whether or not you're loyal, Isaac. I already know the answer to that question. I wouldn't want you to put yourself in a bad position over me," Amber said, clarifying.

"With all due respect, I can decide the risks I'm willing to take." The man's loyalty would never be in question, and Rylan couldn't help thinking that

Isaac would've made a good soldier. He had all the right qualities: honesty, loyalty and bravery. Everything else could be taught.

Amber pursed her lips, no doubt wanting Isaac to think of himself first but obviously realizing he wouldn't. When she finally spoke, she said, "Thank you, Isaac. You're a good man, and you can't know how much I appreciate everything you do for my family."

Isaac allowed himself a small smile before nodding.

Rylan pulled away and navigated around the house toward the barn. Between family members and ranch hands, there were enough vehicles at the Kent main house parking lot to slip into a spot and have a reasonable expectation no one would be the wiser.

"There are sleeping quarters in the barn if you'd rather go with the men—"

"I know." He'd worked three summers in that barn alongside his best friend, Will. Damn. Everything good about Rylan's childhood always came back to the Kent family—a family that had always made him feel like one of their own despite him being from the wrong side of the tracks, coming from a no-good father and having a decent hardworking mother who had no gas left in the tank to spend time with him on the rare occasions she wasn't at work. "I don't want to be separated from you, Amber. Not right now."

Amber gave a small smile before fishing out her

key ring and fanning out the keys. After sliding a couple around the ring, she selected one. "I'll grab a few things from the main house and meet you in the bunkhouse."

The thought of being alone with Brooklyn set his stress levels on high alert. This was his daughter, and he had to learn how to be alone with her. Rylan had been to a hostile country. He'd encountered enemies with every kind of face-to-face weaponry. He'd endured hostile, unforgiving terrain.

But he'd never imagined something that weighed next to nothing would be the thing to take him down.

Rylan brought the whole car seat inside with him. The bunkhouse was actually an apartment over the Kent Ranch offices.

In a few hours, Lonnie would be awake and ready to start the day. It wasn't uncommon for one of the Kents to sleep over in the second-story apartment, so Lonnie most likely wouldn't be the wiser as to who was actually there. He wouldn't bother the occupants.

It didn't seem right to sneak around the same ranch he could practically call home. Being here brought back so many memories, most of them were good. His last year in Jacobstown had been hell after his mother had passed away.

The offices smelled the same, hay and horses. With a diaper bag over his shoulder and a baby carrier in his left hand, he would be a sight. No one from his past would believe this to be possible. Hell, he was still trying to digest this one.

He shuffled up the wooden stairs, looking over the offices where he'd spent so much of his childhood.

The apartment was small but cozy. The furniture was arranged just like he remembered. There was an open-concept living room with a kitchenette. A flat screen was mounted on one wall, with the most comfortable couch Rylan had ever slept on across from it.

The kitchenette was in the corner. This close to the offices and barn it only had a sink, a fridge and a microwave, but that was good enough to get by in a pinch. The apartment was never meant to be a permanent residence. The rectangular dining table had one of its long sides pushed up against the wall. Two chairs were at opposite ends, and two were tucked into the same side. It was comfortable for two, maybe three people to eat there. Four was a stretch even though there were four place settings.

And Rylan had crammed at the table with Will and a couple of ranch hands more than once. Being here reminded him of everything he'd lost, his mother and then his friends, and anger welled up inside him at his past weakness.

He couldn't help but glance down at his daughter and feel nothing but pain at the fact she would never meet her grandmother. Had his mother been around for him? No. But she'd worked hard to keep food on the table and never asked for anything in return. As far as Rylan was concerned, the woman was a saint. It mattered little that he didn't really know her. He loved her the same. Losing her had sent him into a downward spiral that had cost him everything he cared about, and most of his self-confidence.

The door opened and Amber slipped inside carrying a full armload of baby items.

"That was quick," he said, ignoring the way his heart fisted when he saw her again, and how much he didn't want to think about her but did while she was gone.

The kiss they'd shared on that couch had been out of nowhere and one he'd never forget as long as he lived. She'd turned to him, locked gazes and then pressed her lips to his. He should've stopped her and eventually he did. But not before a bone-searing kiss that left him wanting more than he could allow.

"I knew where everything was." Before she could finish her sentence, he was by her side, helping her unload the supplies. She had a smaller and softer version of the baby carrier. She set it up next to the couch. "When she wakes and has a feeding, which should be any minute now, we'll change her and move her to where she'll be more comfortable."

Rylan stood by helpless as she unfolded the cloth seat and opened the straps, so it would be ready for Brooklyn.

"Dinner's in that bag," she continued. "I grabbed a pan of Joyce's lasagna from the fridge."

"I miss her cooking," he said.

"Heat it up and I'll get everything ready over here." This wasn't the time for old memories. Rylan knew better than to allow Amber's voice to roll over him like it was. He knew better than to think about the kiss they'd shared. And he especially knew better than to compare it to all the others since, because they came nowhere close to matching until she'd kissed him again the other day.

Amber Kent proved to be trouble he didn't need in his already overcomplicated life. Damn that life could change with the snap of a finger. It had been like that when he'd lost his mother and had caught him completely off guard.

Being here on the Kent property, Rylan couldn't help but remember the past—a part of his past that he wasn't exactly proud of. He wouldn't go back and change it if he could, mistakes and all. It had made him a better person. It had made him the man he was today. The kind of man who would step up and take care of his responsibilities no matter what else it cost him. A man who wouldn't think twice about offering a helping hand to anyone in need.

Amber's words from earlier started to take root. Maybe he hadn't taken that first drink. Rylan hoped like hell that was true because if he had, that said there'd been no change in him, no growth, and after everything he'd been through to earn his sobriety, he didn't want that to be true.

Brooklyn started to cry, and Amber went right to her while he fixed a bottle. They were getting pretty damn good at parenting together, and he couldn't imagine doing any of this without her. Reality was a gut punch. Because once this ordeal was over, she'd go back to her life here on the ranch and he'd go back to his. For the first time, he felt unsettled about his decision to come back to Jacobstown. But where else would he go?

He chalked his feelings up to not facing the Willow family yet. It was part of his commitment to his sobriety to apologize to those he'd hurt in the past. He'd saved the Willows for last along with Will. Facing those two was going to be the most difficult, and he'd wanted to be strong.

Amber fed his daughter while he set the table.

Rylan's cell buzzed, and he stopped long enough to answer. "What's going on, Zach?"

"I did some digging around into Mr. Robinson's business—"

"Hold on a sec while I put you on speaker," Rylan interrupted. He moved to the couch and sat on the arm while holding out the cell between him and Amber while she burped the baby. "Amber's here.

You were saying that you poked around in Mr. Robinson's business?"

"That's right. It turns out that Alicia Ward was one of his employees. She left almost a year ago," Zach informed them.

"That would be around the time Alicia got pregnant." Amber looked up at Rylan, and his fingers flexed and released from wanting to touch her.

"There've been domestic violence and assault claims against Mr. Robinson by his wife and a woman by the name of Charlotte Pemberton. I traced her to an escort service out of Dallas. Most of the claims came from his wife, but she dropped each one. It's the same story for Ms. Pemberton," Zach said.

A picture emerged that made Rylan's gut twist into a knot.

"Would those cases be enough to stop the Robinsons from being able to adopt a child since they didn't stick?" Amber asked.

"A legitimate adoption agency would have a difficult time getting over physical violence charges. A good interviewer would be able to see right through the Robinsons." Zach paused a beat. "Mr. Robinson also chairs a reelection campaign for the judge who resides over his county. George is influential in Texas."

Several thoughts raced through Rylan's mind. Had Robinson paid Alicia to get pregnant when he and his wife couldn't have a child? And then had Alicia decided not to go through with it? That she couldn't do that to a child? To the man she'd targeted to be the child's father?

"I also found out that Alicia has a sister who lives in Austin. Her name is Adeline. The two were reportedly close until last year. Adeline claims not to have seen or heard from her sister in the past six months," Zach stated.

"We know she's alive," Rylan stated. "Or she was. Otherwise, Brooklyn wouldn't be in the world. We know Alicia was alive a few days ago because she fits the description given by Chess."

"That's what I've found out for now. Technically, I can hold Mr. Robinson for seventy-two hours, but that's a risky move. For now, the Robinsons are in my office. I'm treating them like victims rather than suspects. I thought you should know where we stood," Zach said.

"I appreciate it," Rylan offered.

"Zach, before you go. Can I ask a question on a different subject?" Amber asked.

"Go ahead."

"It's about Breanna. With everything that's going on, have you been able to locate her parents?" Amber's voice was low and reverent. Rylan could see the sadness in her eyes when she spoke about the victim.

"No, I haven't. I have a deputy dedicated to searching for them, though," he said.

"Word was that they moved to San Antonio a few years ago." Amber paused a beat. "I'd heard Breanna was back and that she was still using. I know that won't affect how vigorously you work to bring justice to her killer, Zach. I'm just saying we might want to look into that community to see where she's been and who she's been hanging around with lately."

"I'll make a list and start there, Amber. Thanks for the information." Zach's voice was somber.

"You're welcome, Zach. Are we back to the same suspects?"

"Reggie Barstock still tops the list. I'll look for any connection between him and Breanna. There were no signs of a struggle, which leads me to believe she was familiar with her killer." Amber visibly shivered, and Rylan figured it was the thought someone she knew could do something so unimaginable.

"There's one more thing," Zach said. "I had Deputy Perry poke around in Teague Thompson's practice, and he's been associated with illegal adoption rings in the past. The guy is dirty but he's also connected. His uncle is a senator, and their connections in Texas run deep."

"Sounds like one hell of a web," Rylan stated.

"It is, which means we have to build a solid case for you and Brooklyn in order to keep the two of you together. Perry is on his way over to Alicia's sister's house in Austin. Turns out Alicia's laptop is at her sister's place." Zach was a miracle worker and a damn fine investigator once he had a trail to follow. "Hang in there a little longer. I'm tying up the Robinsons here, but I don't have enough evidence to hold them if they decide to walk out the door. If I can support the emerging picture, I'll have enough evidence to make an arrest."

"Any sign of Alicia?" Rylan asked. The unspoken possibility was that Mr. Robinson had already gotten to her and she was already dead.

"Nothing yet but her laptop might give us a few leads," Zach said.

Rylan ended the call after thanking the sheriff for the update.

"I vaguely remember Reggie Barstock growing up. What's the deal with him?" he asked Amber.

"He was Maddie's boy," Amber told him.

"I remember her. Sweet lady." Rylan didn't know the family very well, and he had no memories of Reggie. "She had that business downtown for the longest time."

"That's right," Amber agreed. "All I remember about Reggie is that he stuck to himself in school. He didn't play any sports, and I don't remember him being much of a student. I think Deacon was a little surprised he graduated from high school. My brother said there'd been some talk of Reggie being held back for grades or absences. Maddie Barstock was a saint.

No one could figure out how Reggie had turned out so opposite except that he'd had a no-good father. You know how the town can be once they lock on to something. Anyway, his mom's reputation was golden, and she'd been a kind employer to everyone who'd worked for her. She passed away last year and left Reggie out of the will. Ms. Barstock left everything to her grandniece, Chelsea."

Rylan perked up at hearing the name. "The same one I met at your home the other day?" he asked.

"That's her. She's an amazing person, and she owns the craft pizza restaurant on the town square." Amber practically beamed with pride. She'd always been all about family. But then the Kents were a tight-knit bunch. Rylan had seen it firsthand even though he'd learned to appreciate so much more now that he was a grown man.

"I'm sure Reggie didn't take too kindly to what he would view as his inheritance going to someone he didn't know," Rylan concluded.

"It was strange knowing he'd been slipping in and out of town without anyone seeing him. Zach found out last year and since Reggie has a limp on his left side—"

"Those are easy dots to connect, considering you said it was always the left paw or hoof. And now Breanna's left foot was—"

She flashed her eyes at him like she could hear the

details even though they both knew what had happened because of the crime scene photos.

"So, yeah, the guy disappeared after high school and most had believed him to be gone for good. He resurfaced last year full of bitterness, and not the least bit sad about his mother's passing. All he seemed to care about was his inheritance. He tried to scare Chelsea into leaving town, which was awful. Apparently, he's been living in Louisiana all this time getting in and out of trouble," she said.

"What kind of crimes was he committing?" Rylan asked.

"Zach said it was small-time stuff. But everyone agrees that he needs to be watched. I mean, he knows Jacobstown, having grown up here. And, sure, a picture has been emerging that he's the one, but Zach isn't convinced yet. No one can reconcile the fact that he didn't come across as the smartest guy, and the profile of the Jacobstown Hacker indicates someone with a higher IQ." She blew out a breath in frustration, and he realized how taxing it was for her to talk about this.

Brooklyn started fussing, and before he could react Amber was at the little girl's side. It was a good time for him to think about getting a meal into Amber and making sure she got rest. He could see that she took care of everyone around her. But who took care of her?

"The baby's settled," Amber announced with pride that stirred places in his heart he thought long since dead. He'd been dead inside far too long.

"Come eat." He'd set the table, and the lasagna smelled damn near out of this world.

Amber joined him and took her seat. Tired and frazzled, she was still beautiful. She must've been starved because she didn't say a word until she'd cleared half her plate. Rylan liked watching her enjoy a good meal. There were other things he liked about her that he didn't want to focus on.

"I know Joyce is an amazing cook but this food is beyond good," Amber said. The sound of appreciation in her voice stirred his heart.

Rylan glanced down at his empty plate with a forced smile. "Like I said, I haven't had this good of a meal in longer than I can remember."

"I'm going to finish eating, take a shower and then I want to talk about why that is, Rylan."

Chapter Sixteen

Rylan made a pot of coffee. He'd been successfully avoiding the topic of his and Will's blowout up until now, but he figured he owed Amber an explanation. She deserved to know the reason because he could see an emotion stir behind her eyes that he hadn't been able to pinpoint until now. It finally dawned on him that she blamed herself, that kiss, for him running off to join the military. So, she most likely blamed herself for the fight between him and Will.

He'd showered in the spare bathroom downstairs while Amber used the one in the apartment. He knew his way around the Kent Ranch, so it was easy to navigate even with little lighting. He also knew where all the supplies were stocked. He'd found an extra set of clothes that roughly fit, brushed his teeth and had settled at the table with his first cup when Amber emerged from the bathroom.

Her hair was down. It fell well past her shoulders. She had on a Grateful Dead T-shirt and shorts that were almost hidden by the oversize tee. Her long legs looked silky and smooth. He clenched and released his hands. Then, he picked up his coffee mug and forced his gaze away from her attributes. After taking a sip, he stood up. "You want a cup?"

"Stay right where you are, Rylan. I'll get it." She shot a smile that was a dagger to his heart. It was difficult to maintain objectivity when she was in the room and everything about her was temptation.

After pouring her cup and doctoring it up, she joined him at the table.

"You should probably get some rest," he said to her.

"I highly doubt if I could. I keep thinking about Breanna and what happened. And then this situation, the uncertainty... Besides, if I'm really that tired, I could drink a cup of coffee on my way to bed and still sleep," she said with a half smile. It didn't reach her eyes and he knew why.

"You want to talk about it?" He liked talking to Amber even though he was normally the silent type.

"I know you and my brother got into a fight but you left and never looked back. I didn't think I'd see you again." Her voice hitched and her cheeks flushed as though the admission, the sadness, embarrassed her.

When she looked up at him with a mix of hurt and defeat in her eyes, his heart fisted in his chest.

"I'm sorry I disappeared on you," he admitted. "My life had spiraled down a bad path and…"

"Was it because you kissed me? Because I've been thinking about that night here in the apartment a lot lately and it was my fault, Rylan. You didn't kiss me. I distinctly remember that I kissed you." Suddenly, the rim of her coffee mug became very interesting to her. Her cheeks flushed with what looked like embarrassment, and he'd be damned if it didn't make her look even more beautiful.

"There was so much more to it than that," he said, hating that she'd carried a sense of shame with her all these years. "My life became a mess. That's why I kissed you back and—"

"Oh. You don't have to explain—"

"Hang on. I didn't mean it to come out like that," he said, backpedaling. "What I'm trying to say is that there are lines that shouldn't be crossed. Kissing your best friend's little sister behind his back is not exactly a stand-up thing to do. Mine and your brother's relationship was already strained. I had no right to do that."

Amber stood, picked up her dish and silverware from earlier, and said, "You don't need to defend yourself."

"Is that what you think I'm doing?" He stood and followed her into the kitchenette where there was barely room for one.

She turned on the faucet and rinsed her plate, keeping her back to him. The only time she ever did something like that was when she was too angry or too embarrassed to talk, and his heart took a hit thinking he'd caused her reaction.

He'd gone and made a mess of the situation.

"Amber—"

"Don't, Rylan. I'm not in the mood to be insulted by the person I'm in the middle of helping. A person who won't tell me why he won't sleep inside the main house. A person who disappeared into the military after a blowout with my brother and never looked back and won't tell me what happened in the first place." She kept her back to him as she stood in front of the sink.

"You think I walked away and never looked back?" He was so close behind her that her flowery scent filled his senses. He could reach out and touch her, so he did. He put his hands on her shoulders and felt her skin heat a little under his touch. Her body's reaction to him stirred an already awake part of his anatomy that was difficult to hide underneath jogging shorts.

"Isn't that what you did, Rylan? Isn't that what you're going to do as soon as the dust settles again and you get bored or whatever it was that caused you to go to Collinsville in the first place? Isn't that exactly how you got into trouble before?" Her words rushed out like they did when she was stressed.

He took a step closer and was almost body to body. It was taking all his self-control not to reach out and touch her. It would be so easy to move her hair away from her neck and start kissing her there.

Before he could drum up the willpower to turn away, she took a step back and leaned against him.

Rylan had to admit his feelings for Amber were always brimming underneath the surface. Seeing her with his child did things to his heart that he knew better than to allow. He had no business falling for a Kent.

Honestly, she was too good for him but she'd never see it that way.

"Are you going to answer me?" Her pulse drummed underneath his fingertips.

"What can I tell you, Amber? Do you want to hear that I think you're beautiful? That you make me want things that I don't deserve? That I will never deserve and, by the way, your brother agreed with me? Because I'll say it. And then what? You'll feel sorry for me—"

Amber spun around with all that ire in her eyes that was so damn sexy. "I couldn't possibly feel sorry for you, Rylan. As far as my brother goes, he has no idea what's best for me."

This close, her body was flush with his, and he

could feel her breasts rising and falling when she spoke. He dropped his hands, looping his arms around her waist. All he could feel right then was the desire sweeping through him, consuming him with need.

"All I can feel is the same thing you do." Looking into her glittery eyes wasn't helping his situation any.

"This is a bad idea," he said.

AMBER BROUGHT HER hands up to Rylan's chest and smoothed her fingers over the ridges beneath his T-shirt. She blinked up at him. "Is this a bad idea, Rylan? Because I can't think of one good reason why this shouldn't happen. We're adults now. Adults who are capable of making the decision to have one night of amazing sex together."

She pushed up on her tiptoes and kissed him. His body went rigid at first, but then he pulled her tighter against him.

"I won't deny that you've grown up, Amber. You're incredible. You're smart. Beautiful," he said.

Pulling back, she looked directly into his eyes and realized just how much trouble she was in. The more time she spent with Rylan, Amber could sense herself falling further down that slippery slope of feelings. The heat that had been burning between them was like nothing she'd ever felt in her past relationships.

Their chemistry sizzled, and she assumed the sex would be beyond anything she'd ever experienced.

It would be so easy to get lost with this man in this moment and forget about the past, about their history.

And that's exactly what she planned to do for at least one night.

She dropped her hands to the hem of Rylan's T-shirt while locking gazes with him. His hands joined hers, and a few seconds later his shirt was on the floor.

His hands went to the hem of hers, and her fingers trembled with anticipation as she fumbled with the fabric, trying to help. He captured one of her hands in his and brought it up to his lips. He pressed a kiss on the tip of her fingers and then on her palm. He peppered kisses on her exposed wrist. Sensual shivers skittered across her skin and her stomach went into free fall.

"I said it before and I'll say it again—you're beautiful, Amber Kent." His voice was low, raspy and sexy as hell. "You're even more beautiful than I remembered, and that's saying a hell of a lot."

He pulled her T-shirt up and over her head, and it joined his shirt on the floor. He palmed her breasts and she released a moan as she unhooked her lacy bra. His hands were rough from working on his house. She liked the feel of them against her skin as they roamed.

He toed off his boots and she followed suit.

"Why did you disappear after you kissed me?" She couldn't help but ask the question that had been on her mind far too long.

"You really want to talk about this now?" He ran his finger along the waistband of her shorts. "Because I have something else entirely on my mind, and it's a hell of a lot better than dredging up the past. It's the here and now, you and me. And I've been waiting a long time for the chance to do this."

He sure knew the right things to say as he dipped his head and ran his lips across her collarbone and then along the base of her neck. Warmth coiled low in her belly.

"It can wait." She wanted this to happen, this thing that was happening between them. She wanted it more than she wanted air.

Maybe she was caught up in the moment, but she didn't care. She'd denied herself too long. She moved her hands to the waistband of his shorts, and a few seconds later those were on the floor in a pile with their clothes. Her shorts joined his.

He hooked his thumbs on either side of her panties, and those went on top of the pile along with his boxers.

Rylan Anderson stood there, naked, and in front of her. His glorious body glistening in the moonlight streaming in from the top of the window. Shadows highlighted a strong male body. His erection pressed against the soft skin of her belly when he pulled her close to him. Again, their bodies were flush and she could feel every time he took a breath.

How many times had she wished for this when she was still naive enough to believe in wishes? One of the biggest problems with her relationship with Red was that he wasn't Rylan, would never be Rylan. She'd told herself to get over her crush and move on. And she believed she had until now. Now she realized she'd just stuffed her feelings down so deep that she'd become numb.

She brought her hands up and dug her fingers into his thick hair and breathed. Her breasts pressed against him as his hands roamed around her back and then cradled her bottom. A thunderclap of need exploded inside her and all she could think about was this man, his weight on top of her, pressing her deeper into the mattress.

Amber had no idea the air could heat up so quickly or the chemistry between two people could be so explosive until Rylan. She'd call it attraction or chemistry, but there was so much more to it than physical. Although, he was one damn hot man. With Rylan, there was a deeper connection.

He lifted her up and she wrapped her legs around his toned midsection. She could feel his erection pulsing against her heat. With her arms around him and his hands cupping her bottom, he walked her into the bedroom and set her down on top of the covers.

It took less than a minute to retrieve a condom and sheath his stiff length before Amber wrapped her arms around his neck and kissed him. His response? He kissed her so thoroughly that if she wasn't already on the bed, her legs might have given out from underneath her. He cupped her breasts with his right palm as he balanced most of his weight on his left hand. Her nipple beaded as he rolled it between this thumb and finger, teasing her. Her back arched and she let out a mewl.

He captured it with his mouth.

"I want to feel you moving inside me, Rylan," Amber coaxed.

It didn't take much encouragement.

He pinned her to the mattress with his heft, careful not to overwhelm her with his weight. She wrapped her legs around his midsection and he drove his tip inside her heat. For the first few seconds he just teased her, driving her to the brink of craziness.

Amber bucked her hips as she dug her fingers into Rylan's shoulders. He drove himself deeper inside her as he lowered his head and captured her mouth. He tasted like a mix of coffee and peppermint toothpaste.

Bare skin to bare skin, he groaned as he thrust

harder and faster. She matched his pitch as they practically gasped for air.

His stiff erection drove to her core, and she rode the feeling to the brink. Faster. Harder. More.

"Rylan," she rasped.

He pulled his head back far enough to really look at her. "You're incredible, Amber."

She loved the sound of her name as it rolled off his tongue. She heard something else that sounded a lot like, "I love you." But she was probably just hearing what she wanted as he pushed her over the edge and rocketed her toward climax.

It was then he drove himself faster and harder until his entire body tensed…and then sweet release seemed to wash over him as he let out a guttural groan.

Rylan collapsed alongside her. She rolled onto her side to face him, and he pulled her into the crook of his arm. He kissed her again and she memorized the look on his face. It was the first time she could remember seeing him with a smile that lit his eyes. It was addicting and dangerous, making the pull to him even stronger.

"Amber Kent, I hope you're not tired because one time is not nearly enough with you."

Chapter Seventeen

Making love with Amber changed things for Rylan. Now that he'd cracked the lid on that pot, he could only hope she felt the same. Lying there, skin to skin with her, he knew he was only beginning to scratch the surface of his feelings for her.

Amber's steady, even breathing said she was asleep, and he didn't want to disturb her. Brooklyn would be awake soon, needing another bottle. He peeled himself away from Amber and out from under the covers, moving slowly and quietly so as not to disturb her. She needed rest. If she heard the baby, she'd hop up before he could throw his shorts on.

Rylan walked into the kitchenette area and put on a pot of coffee. There was no way he could sleep thinking that Brooklyn's mother might already be dead. His mother had passed away while he was in high school, but looking back as a man he was nothing but grateful for the time he got with her.

It was taking all of Rylan's self-control to stop

himself from going down to Zach's office and forcing the smug Mr. Robinson to talk. The sheriff had laws to follow whereas Rylan had better ways to make the man talk. And if the Robinsons weren't still there, he'd hunt them down. But then, he hadn't let his temper rule him since those bad decisions he'd made in high school. He'd finally realized letting his temper control his actions hurt him and the people he cared most about in the long run. But times like these tried his patience, and a woman's life could hang in the balance.

Patience had never been his strong suit.

He was deep into his second cup of coffee when Brooklyn stirred. Staring down a baby alone was enough to make this strong man crumble.

But he was nothing but proud when he made her bottle, fed her and burped her, before changing her diaper. Since he'd acted fast the little girl had never properly woken up and that made changing her diaper a hell of a lot easier. He had Amber to thank for helping him get the hang of things.

Pride filled his chest when he placed her back inside her infant bouncer and successfully strapped her in. For the first time since having her handed to him out of the blue, he was starting to think he might not be awful at caring for her.

It was even better that Amber was still sleeping. The thought of being her shelter and taking care of her stirred his heart. Not that Amber Kent couldn't take care of herself. It was sexy as hell when a strong woman could open herself up and allow herself to be vulnerable. And he liked the feeling of taking care of someone who did so much for others.

Rylan thought about Mr. Robinson. A picture emerged that made him sick to his stomach. Had Alicia been forced—or pressured might be a better word—into having a child for her boss? A man with his temperament and dominant tendencies would see no problem in forcing one of his employees to do something she didn't want to. If the man didn't treat the woman he was supposed to love above all else with respect, how was he supposed to treat people he would see as pawns?

There were other thoughts that popped into Rylan's mind. Why did Alicia have a change of heart? Although, looking at the way Amber had almost instantly bonded with Brooklyn, he figured there was a built-in protection hormone for mothers. Had Alicia bonded with the baby during the pregnancy? He'd heard about rogue hormones in pregnant women. They served a purpose, and he figured most of them were to ensure survival of the child.

Thinking about Zach's phone call earlier got Rylan's mind spinning. He wasn't quite ready to let himself off the hook about the slip last year in his sobriety. Evidence was mounting that Alicia might've been desperate to get pregnant. She could've locked on to him after seeing him at the party. And she could've slipped something into his coffee.

Until he had proof, Rylan couldn't afford to let himself off.

He grabbed a small notebook and pen from the junk drawer in the kitchenette, and then started jotting down notes.

By the time he looked up fifteen minutes later, Amber stood in the doorway to the bedroom staring at him.

"Hello, beautiful," he said, and she broke into a smile.

"Rylan." Her voice had a tentative quality to it, and he figured he knew why.

"You're important to me, Amber. Last night changed things for me. I just don't know what that means yet," he offered, and thought he saw a flicker of disappointment behind her eyes as she approached.

He grabbed her hand and tugged her down onto his lap. He kissed her, wishing he could say what was really on his mind, that he'd had a hell of a time going all-in with anyone. But the thought of losing Amber was a knife stab to the center of his chest.

The sound of boots shuffling up wooden stairs had Rylan reaching for his weapon. Amber immediately went toward the baby.

"Will you take her into the bedroom?" She had her SIG and could protect them both given the time.

"Be careful, Rylan."

"Close the door but wait to see who opens it before you shoot." He fired a wink and it was meant to break the tension.

She frowned.

"Don't count me out yet, Kent. I'm actually damn good in these situations."

Amber smiled but it didn't reach her eyes. Worry lines creased her forehead as she picked up the baby in her bouncer and glanced back one more time before closing the door. He could've sworn she whispered that she loved him, but it could've been his imagination.

A knock sounded.

"It's Will. Open up."

The bedroom door cracked open. "I'll let the two of you talk while I hang out with this sweet girl."

Amber stood there holding Brooklyn in her arms. The baby smiled up at Amber. And a fire bolt struck Rylan square in the chest.

He walked to the door and answered. "How'd you know I was here?"

"Where's my sister? Is she safe?" Will's concern touched Rylan. Although, he shouldn't be surprised a Kent would look out for another Kent.

"She's here." Rylan opened the door all the way. "You want to come inside?"

Will glanced at him before nodding.

"A lot has happened since we last spoke." Rylan motioned toward the table. "You want a cup of coffee?"

The sun wasn't up yet, but days started on the ranch at 4:00 a.m. Rylan should've known they couldn't fool her family, thinking they could go unnoticed on the property.

"I'll take a cup if you've got it. Black." Will took a seat.

Rylan poured two and joined Will. He set down one of the mugs in front of his former best friend.

"Before you say anything, I'd like to apologize to you," Rylan began.

"There's no reason to rehash the—"

"I believe there is. And it's an important step in my sobriety."

Will's eyes widened in surprise.

"That's right. I've been sober for many years now, but facing you has been the most difficult part of the journey," Rylan admitted.

"Why is that?" Will took a sip and studied Rylan's face.

"I needed to be ready to forgive myself if you accepted my apology. And I'm not there yet but—"

"Losing a friendship, hell, a brotherhood has been punishment enough. Don't you think?" The sincerity in Will's words struck like a physical blow.

Had he missed the friendship as much as Rylan?

"You covered for me that night. What I did was wrong, and you stuck up for me even though I didn't deserve it. I was a stupid kid—"

"You lost your mother, and I couldn't seem to help pick you back up or get you on the right path again," Will said.

"I let you down, not the other way around. And I let the Willow family down by catching their crops on fire." Saying those words still hurt. "I had no business—"

"Hold on a second. You think it was *you* who lit that fire?" Will's voice was steady.

"I was the one there. You said it yourself. That's where you found me. You took the blame so I wouldn't end up in juvenile detention." That's how Rylan remembered it.

"The McFarland boys set that fire, and they did it on purpose. I just couldn't prove it. They were drunk and seemed to think it would be real funny to destroy the field. You were passed out. I found you before the flames got to you, or they would've let you die. I was angry with you at the time for choosing those jerks over our friendship. You never had anything to do with the fire. My parents helped the Willows get back on their feet. But you almost lost your life." Will smacked his palm on the table. "I was almost too late that night, but it never should've gone that far. I should've been a better friend."

Rylan let those words sink in. All the guilt he'd been feeling these years for the fire had been wasted? Damn, those were a lot of years to be carrying around shame for something he didn't do. Looking back, they'd been for nothing.

He didn't regret his time in the military. He'd gotten his act together there. His service had been good for him. "Thank you for telling me, Will."

"I tried to talk to you before you left, but you said you didn't want to look back."

If only he'd known. "Being stubborn isn't my best trait."

Will chuckled and it broke the tension. "You think?"

"I'm sorry for the pain I caused, man. I missed our friendship. It's one of the main reasons I decided to straighten up my act."

"That means a lot to hear." Will offered a handshake. "How about we pick up where we left off, but from the good times?"

"Now that's a deal." Rylan took the hand being offered. "For the record, I had no idea I was getting your sister into a mess when I called her the other day for help." Those words couldn't be truer.

Will didn't respond right away. He seemed to take a minute to think. "I realize you would never put my sister in harm's way."

"She means a lot to me, Will."

"I saw that the other day. That's why I walked outside to clear my head. I'd imagined a different scenario happening if you and me were ever in the same room again." Will's face brightened. "It involved fists."

"Yeah, I deserve it after the way I messed things up in our friendship," Rylan said.

"Well, I thought you'd be throwing the first punch," Will admitted.

"I guess I had a lot of pent-up aggression in high school." Rylan took a sip of coffee. "The only punch I want to throw now is at the person who's trying to take my daughter away."

He updated Will on the situation with Alicia and the Robinsons.

"Zach promised to call when he got further into the investigation." Rylan set his mug down. He looked up at Will. "Your sister's in the other room if you want to talk to her."

"I don't have anything to say, except take it easy on her. She went through a lot and, strong as she is, none of us want to see her hurting like that again. It nearly cracked us in half when we saw her after she lost the baby. Her son-of-a-bitch ex took off, not that she ever cared about him the way she does about you." Will lasered a look at Rylan. "You do realize my sister has feelings for you, right?"

"I hope so." Rylan sure as hell had feelings for her. What that meant in the long run, he had no idea. Right now, all he could think about was putting Mr.

Robinson behind bars and making sure that both Amber and Brooklyn were safe. For his daughter's sake, he needed to find her mother.

"Good. Because even when she was married I never saw her look at him like she does you." Those words broke through the walls he'd carefully constructed.

"The truth is, Will, I'm not nearly good enough for your sister." He kept his tone church-quiet because he knew she'd argue if she heard.

"You know what, buddy? There was a time when I would've blindly agreed with that statement. Not anymore. For what it's worth, I think you're exactly who she needs." Will set his mug down and stood up. He turned toward the cracked bedroom door. "Did you hear that, Amber?"

"I sure did," she said with all that stubbornness and ire he loved about her.

Will left and Amber walked into the room.

"We need to talk," she said. "Later."

Rylan wasn't sure he liked the uncertainty in her tone. Was she shutting down on him? Was this— whatever *this* meant—moving too fast? He felt caught up in a rogue wave. For now, he was riding on top but how long before it sucked him under and tossed him out to sea?

AMBER HELD BROOKLYN to her chest. She couldn't allow this angel to cloud her judgment and yet how could she not? Holding this baby felt so right. Being with Rylan felt so right. But what didn't feel so right was the fact that Amber wasn't Brooklyn's mother.

Boots shuffled up the stairs and Amber's gaze went to the table, searching for whatever it was that Will forgot. She made a move toward the door, but it swung open and Mr. Robinson stood at the entrance.

Amber stared at the barrel of a gun.

"Hold on there, buddy," Rylan said. His cell buzzed on the table.

"Come over here," Mr. Robinson ordered. His eyes wild and angry, he looked like a hungry predator closing in on prey.

Amber was paralyzed with fear. All she could do was hold the baby tighter to her chest. If danger involved only her, she wouldn't hesitate to fight back or try to duck for cover. But holding the baby ensured Amber would move slower. A half-second hesitation could give Mr. Robinson the upper hand. Damned if he didn't already have it, and that just burned Amber up inside. She'd never played the victim role and had no plans to start now. She would, however, do whatever was necessary in order to ensure Brooklyn's safety.

Rylan was near the table on the opposite side of the sofa. His cell was buzzing madly on the table. Even a skilled soldier like him couldn't make that leap before Mr. Robinson got off a shot.

"You don't want her," Rylan interrupted. "I'm the one you want."

Mr. Robinson's hand trembled, and she could almost visibly see his blood pressure rise. "I'll decide who's going with me."

"Where's the baby's mother?" Rylan asked.

"She's not coming back." Robinson's face twisted when he said the words. "I killed her with my own hands. Stupid bitch couldn't follow simple directions. All she had to do was have the baby and hand her over. I would've preferred a son. Women are so weak. But my wife wanted her anyway."

Amber glanced at Rylan, half expecting him to make a move but knowing he couldn't. Her heart ached for how calloused this man sounded about taking Brooklyn's mother's life. No matter how bad of a mother Alicia might've been or undeserving of this angel, the woman didn't deserve to have her life cut short.

Amber was close to the door. The gun was pointed at *her.*

There was no way she'd allow this man to shoot the baby. Amber turned to block Brooklyn and give Mr. Robinson a clear shot at her instead.

"It's okay, Rylan," Amber said in as calm a voice as she could muster. If anyone made a wrong move, Mr. Robinson could get spooked and pull the trigger.

"No one told you to speak," Mr. Robinson seethed.

Didn't those words grate on Amber. This man needed to wake up. It wasn't 1950 anymore. Women could vote. They could run ranches and have a variety of careers. And, at least in her case, could shoot a gun. So, he'd better watch his mouth.

"If anything happens to me, you won't get what you came for." Amber motioned toward the baby. "I go down and I take her with me. You lose. You'll be arrested. My cousin, Zach McWilliams, won't sleep or stop until he hunts you down. So, it seems we're in a bit of a stalemate."

"Her cousin might go after you legally, but I'll go after your family. Your wife. Your mother. Any living relative you hold dear. And then I'll come after you. You'll know it's coming. It's going to happen but you won't know when and you sure as hell won't be able to stop me." Rylan's voice was a study in calm composure.

"You'll come with me and bring the baby with you." Mr. Robinson practically spat the words. His voice was filled with the tension of a man on the edge.

And then he shifted the barrel of the gun toward Rylan and fired.

Chapter Eighteen

Rylan was hit. He made a show of flying backward and landing hard against the back wall. He dropped onto the dining table and then rolled off of it. The bastard had to pay. No matter what Alicia had done, she didn't deserve to lose her life. He, of all people, knew what it was like to make mistakes. There should be second chances and not the finality of death.

Amber gasped. The horrific look on her face slammed guilt into him. Yes, he'd taken a bullet, but he'd been in worse tactical situations. A good soldier could detach emotionally and stay logical. So, he'd gone back to his training the minute he realized Robinson was going to walk out the door with Amber and Brooklyn.

Playing up his injury gave him an advantage when there weren't many to be had.

Robinson pushed Amber out the door, and the look of horror on her face would keep Rylan awake at night if his plan failed. It would be the last time he saw her if he didn't play his cards right.

The minute Robinson got Amber into the stairwell, Rylan jumped into action. He moved stealth-like toward the window behind the kitchen sink. He opened it, climbed on top of the counter and slipped out.

Hanging on to the outside of the window, he was able to cut some of the distance to the ground. He'd landed behind the offices. Damn, the sun was coming up, and that meant Lonnie and the ranch hands would be out on the property.

Where was Will?

Fire shot through him at the possibility that anything had happened to his friend. No, that wasn't possible. Rylan and Amber would've heard something. Robinson must've hid in the shadows and waited.

Blood dripped from his left wrist where the bullet had grazed him. Even one-handed he could take down Robinson.

Rylan moved along the shrubbery line at a healthy clip until he saw movement. Robinson had Amber's elbow in his grip. Seeing that shot more fire through Rylan.

He dropped and crouched low so he'd stay below Robinson's line of sight through the brush. He caught his first break when he saw that Robinson was walking Amber toward Rylan's position. The man was a hothead and not a career criminal. All Rylan had to do was exercise patience and wait for the man to slip up.

With a useless left hand, Rylan would have to rely on his right. It wasn't his dominant hand anyway, but one hand down wasn't ideal in any fight. He didn't doubt his skills. Emotions had gotten the best of him in the apartment. How could they not? It was Amber and his child, a child he didn't know about last week and now couldn't imagine living without. The little bean had wiggled her way into his heart.

Steady, Rylan controlled his burst of adrenaline. Part of it came from the pain in his left wrist and the other part was due to the circumstance unfolding. He couldn't allow himself to consider any other outcome than a successful mission. And yet his heart was engaged. It was too late for going all-logic and no-emotion. Which was funny because Rylan had never been one to get caught up in emotion.

Guess he was a changed man now that he could see a future. And his future involved Amber and the baby in her arms, if Amber would have him.

He'd work double time to make up for the loss of Alicia in Brooklyn's life.

Robinson drew near and Rylan caught his second break. The man's nerves were getting to him. It was possible he'd never shot anyone before. Although, he'd admitted to killing Alicia. Was that big talk for a small man?

Rylan had no doubt that Alicia was gone, but one of Robinson's henchmen might've done it. Most people who'd actually taken another life found no need to brag about it.

As the increasingly nervous man looked from side to side, he let the gun barrel point away from Amber.

In a split second, Rylan leaped out of the brush and tackled Robinson before the man's brain could send a message to his finger to pull the trigger.

Rylan disarmed Robinson with ease, knocking the gun loose and causing it to tumble a few feet away onto the grass. It fired and he heard Amber scream.

"Take Brooklyn away from here," Rylan said to Amber. He wanted both of them as far away as possible.

Engaging in death rolls to disorient Robinson, Rylan stopped when he was on top of the older man and squeezed his arms to his sides with the force of his thighs. He might've been one wrist down, but his legs were far more powerful.

Robinson tried to buck, but Rylan just smiled down at the man.

Amber was already shouting for help.

"You're going to spend the rest of your pitiful life behind bars. You're going to make new friends with that winning personality of yours. And if one of your henchmen so much as drives through this county, he won't drive back out alive. Are we clear?" Rylan reared a fist back and punched the jerk who'd killed the mother of Rylan's child and had almost killed the love of his life.

When he looked up at Amber, he saw her handing over the baby to her cousin Amy. And then he saw a red dot flowering on Amber's shirt. What? When?

The next few moments moved as though in slow motion. A security team descended on the scene in less than a minute. Isaac pressed his knee into Robinson's back as he zip-cuffed him.

Rylan flew to Amber the second Robinson had been secured.

Nothing in Rylan's life made sense without Amber. He dropped to her side on the green turf.

"Don't you leave me," he said to her. "I love you, Amber. I *need* you." Rogue tears broke free and fell from his eyes. "Please, stay with me."

Her eyes fluttered and a ghost of a smile crossed her purple lips. She was losing a lot of blood. He pulled up her T-shirt and saw a bullet wound the size of his fist where the bullet exited. Rylan wasn't a religious man, but he cupped her face in his hands and said a protection prayer that he'd learned as a kid.

He vaguely heard crying in the background along with shouting.

"Come on, Amber."

When she didn't respond, he took off his own

shirt, balled it up using his good hand and gently pressed it into her wound to try to stem the bleeding.

"I need an ambulance," he shouted as the shirt was almost immediately soaked.

Rylan couldn't be sure how long it took for the EMTs to arrive on the scene. Time slowed to a standstill as Amber lay on the grass. She had a pulse, but her breathing was shallow.

And his heart nearly stopped beating in his chest.

The EMTs went to work immediately, giving Amber oxygen. They put pressure on the wound and stabilized her enough for her to be transported to County General, which was a twenty-minute drive.

On the way, Will instructed Rylan to pull a shirt out of the gym bag in the back seat. Rylan did as instructed. Pulling it over his head with one hand was tricky, but he managed.

The ambulance driver made it in half that time as Rylan followed. Will had practically dragged him to his vehicle. And then he'd chased that ambulance all the way to the hospital.

Will offered reassurances along the way, but the words were as hollow as the space in Rylan's chest. He pulled into the ambulance bay at the ER. "Go. I'll park and be right up."

"Thank you." Rylan tore out of the passenger seat and was next to the EMT as he brought Amber's gurney out the back of the ambulance.

Lights blared, twisting together as Rylan followed Amber inside. A team waited for her, and he figured that wasn't a good sign under the circumstances.

"Sir, are you hurt?" The intake nurse seemed to notice the blood all over his arm and wrist. Some belonged to Amber and some was his own. The nurse's gaze landed on his wrist as he favored it. No amount of pain could distract him from why he was really there.

"I'm fine. This isn't my blood."

The nurse cocked a concerned eyebrow.

"I'm Ophelia and I'd like to take a look at that wrist if you'll allow it," the nurse said.

"The only person who needs treatment is behind those doors. When can I get an update about her condition?" he asked. He was locked on to a target and nothing else mattered.

Will burst through the ER doors. "I'm with him."

"Any chance you can convince him to accept treatment on his wrist?" Ophelia asked.

"Not until he hears a positive report on my sister, Amber Kent," Will told her.

The last name seemed to register because Ophelia's eyes lit up. "Your family has been so generous to this hospital. Please, follow me."

For once in Rylan's life, he was grateful the Kents had money. He'd sign over his own life savings if it meant getting information about Amber's condition.

"She's brave, Rylan," Will said as Ophelia led them into a private lounge. There were leather chairs instead of hard wooden ones. There was a nice coffee bar off to one side and a fridge with a glass door next to it. Every popular soda was in there along with all the sparkling waters a person could drink.

"Help yourself to a drink or a snack," Ophelia said. "I'll check with the nurse on duty and see if I can get an update for you gentlemen."

Every half hour from that point on, a nurse showed up in the waiting room to talk to Will and Rylan. After two visits, the room was filled with Kents and their spouses. Rylan learned that Brooklyn was safe on the ranch with Joyce, who couldn't stop doting on the little girl. Brooklyn seemed happy as a lark in Joyce's care. She'd been there from day one for Mitch's twins and the other babies as the Kent brood grew.

Zach was the only family member missing, and he was busy arresting Mrs. Robinson for being an accomplice in Alicia's death, a death Zach had confirmed by the coroner's office. He phoned with an update that Alicia's laptop browser had searches for date-rape-type drugs like ketamine. She'd also done research on fentanyl.

Knowing that Rylan had maintained his sobriety felt hollow without Amber to talk to. He missed the sound of her voice, the feel of her skin. He missed her quick wit and even faster smile.

The light that had always been Amber might've dimmed, but in the past twenty-four hours he'd seen it return full force.

After Amber's loved ones waited an agonizing twenty-four hours and she had had three blood transfusions, a nurse walked into the waiting room. Chatter stopped and the room fell silent.

"She's in recovery and she's asking for Rylan Anderson and her brother Will," the nurse announced.

The pair had been hovering over the coffee machine, waiting for news. Rylan had allowed his wrist to be tended to an hour ago once he'd learned that Amber was out of surgery to remove bullet fragments from her hip.

Rylan took the lead and Will followed the nurse down the hall.

"The doctor will be in to speak to the family soon, but he was pleased with how the surgery went," the nurse stated. "She'll be moved into a room soon. He wants to keep her here for a few days to make sure her recovery is smooth."

The middle-aged, short redhead stopped in front of a door. "She's right in here."

Rylan wasted no time walking in, and Will was on his heels.

Amber's eyes were closed. Seeing her in that room

with all the machines beeping and tubes hanging out of her gutted him.

He and Will flanked the bed, and Rylan took her hand in his.

She blinked her eyes open, locked on to Rylan and smiled.

It took another fifteen minutes for her to open her eyes again. This time, she kept them open a little longer.

"Did you mean what you said, Rylan Anderson?" she finally said. She coughed. "My throat is dry as a cactus."

Rylan couldn't help but crack a smile. He picked up a water container and helped her get the straw to her lips.

"Thank you. That's better," she said after taking a drink. "Where's the baby?"

"You gave us a scare," Will said.

"Believe me, I wasn't trying to." The smile faded too soon. "Is everyone else okay? Brooklyn is good, right?"

"Yes. The Robinsons are going to separate prisons where at least Mr. Robinson will spend the rest of his life. Brooklyn is with Joyce, waiting for you to get better so you can hold her again," Rylan said. "And I meant what I said. I love you, Amber. I can't imagine my life without you."

Amber's eyes lit up.

"You heard that, right, Will?" she asked.

Will couldn't help but laugh. "I did."

"Then you can go," she teased.

"I'd like him to stick around if you don't mind," Rylan said, and the room fell quiet from the seriousness of his tone. "Your father was a good man. He was kind to me. I wish he was here all the time, especially now because I'd like to ask him for your hand in marriage. But if Will can step into his father's shoes for a minute, I'll ask him instead."

Will practically beamed as he looked at his sister. Her smile displayed a row of perfectly straight, perfectly white teeth. Not everything was so perfect about Amber, except that she was perfect for Rylan. "Permission granted."

Rylan bent down on one knee. He was still holding on to Amber's hand when he said, "You're my best friend and the first person I want to speak to no matter what kind of day I've had. My heart is yours, Amber. I can't imagine loving anyone more or finding a better partner to spend my life with. So, if you'll do me the honor, I'm asking you to marry me."

"IT's ALWAYS BEEN YOU, Rylan. Ever since that first kiss at sixteen years old I knew there was something special, something that I'd never find with another man." Tears streamed down her cheeks. "So, yes, I'll be your partner, your wife. And I promise to love you with every breath until my last."

Rylan stood up and leaned over the bed to kiss the woman he loved. He finally found where he belonged.

"What do you think about a Valentine's wedding?" Amber asked.

"That's not far off. You sure you don't want time to plan a wedding?"

"I don't want a big wedding. I want a marriage. And I can't think of a better Valentine's present than to make our family official," she said.

Those were all the words he needed to hear. "Valentine's it is."

Will moved around the side of the bed and gripped Rylan in a man hug. "You've always felt like a brother to me. Welcome to the family."

Rylan couldn't think of a better way to spend the rest of his life than with a real family, his daughter and the woman he loved.

* * * * *

Look for What She Saw, *the final book in*
USA TODAY *bestselling author Barb Han's*
Rushing Creek Crime Spree miniseries,
available next month.

And don't miss the previous titles in the series:

Cornered at Christmas
Ransom at Christmas
Ambushed at Christmas
What She Did

Available now from Harlequin Intrigue!

WE HOPE YOU ENJOYED
THIS BOOK FROM

⬙ HARLEQUIN

INTRIGUE

Seek thrills. Solve crimes. Justice served.

Dive into action-packed stories that will keep you
on the edge of your seat. Solve the crime
and deliver justice at all costs.

6 NEW BOOKS AVAILABLE EVERY MONTH!

COMING NEXT MONTH FROM

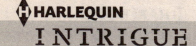

HARLEQUIN

INTRIGUE

Available May 19, 2020

#1929 AMBUSH BEFORE SUNRISE
Cardwell Ranch: Montana Legacy • by B.J. Daniels
Wrangler Angus Savage has come to Wyoming to reconnect with
Jinx McCallahan and help her get her cattle to high country. But when they
set out on the trail, they don't expect to come across so many hazards—
including Jinx's treacherous ex, who wants her back...or dead.

#1930 MIDNIGHT ABDUCTION
Tactical Crime Division • by Nichole Severn
When Benning Reeves's twins are kidnapped, the frantic father asks
Ana Ramirez and the Tactical Crime Division of the FBI for help. As evidence
accumulates, they'll have to discover why this situation connects to an
unresolved case...before it's too late.

#1931 EVASIVE ACTION
Holding the Line • by Carol Ericson
Minutes before her wedding, April Hart learns her fiancé is a drug lord. Now
the only person she can trust is a man from her past—border patrol agent
Clay Archer. April left Clay to protect him from her dangerous family, so this
time Clay is determined to guard April—and his heart.

#1932 WHAT SHE SAW
Rushing Creek Crime Spree • by Barb Han
Deputy Courtney Foster's brief fling with Texas ranch owner Jordan Kent
was her time-out after getting shot in the line of duty. Only now she's
hunting a killer...and she just discovered she's pregnant.

#1933 ISOLATED THREAT
A Badlands Cops Novel • by Nicole Helm
When Cecilia Mills asks sheriff's deputy Brady Wyatt to help her hide a child
from his father's biker gang, Brady will put his life on the line to keep all
three of them safe from the Sons of the Badlands.

#1934 WITHOUT A TRACE
An Echo Lake Novel • by Amanda Stevens
When Rae Cavanaugh's niece mysteriously goes missing, county sheriff
Tom Brannon is determined to find her. But as electricity sparks between
Rae and Tom, Rae discovers—despite her misgivings—Tom is the only one
she can trust...

Prologue

They warned him not to go to the police.

He couldn't think. Couldn't breathe.

Forcing one foot in front of the other, he tried to ignore the gut-
wrenching pain at the base of his skull where the kidnapper had
slammed him into his kitchen floor and knocked him unconscious.
Owen. Olivia. They were out there. Alone. Scared. He hadn't been
strong enough to protect them, but he wasn't going to stop trying to
find them. Not until he got them back.

A wave of dizziness tilted the world on its axis, and he collided
with a wooden street pole. Shoulder-length hair blocked his vision
as he fought to regain balance. He'd woken up a little less than
fifteen minutes ago, started chasing after the taillights of the SUV
as it'd sped down the unpaved road leading into town. He could still
taste the dirt in his mouth. They couldn't have gotten far. Someone
had to have seen something…

Humidity settled deep into his lungs despite the dropping
temperatures, sweat beading at his temples as he pushed himself

upright. Moonlight beamed down on him, exhaustion pulling at every muscle in his body, but he had to keep going. He had to find his kids. They were all he had left. All that mattered.

Colorless worn mom-and-pop stores lining the town's main street blurred in his vision.

A small group of teenagers—at least what looked like teenagers—gathered around a single point on the sidewalk ahead. The kidnapper had sped into town from his property just on the outskirts, and there were only so many roads that would get the bastard out. Maybe someone in the group could point him in the right direction. He latched on to a kid brushing past him by the collar. "Did you see a black SUV speed through here?"

The boy—sixteen, seventeen—shook his head and pulled away. "Get off me, man."

The echo of voices pierced through the ringing in his ears as the circle of teens closed in on itself in front of Sevierville's oldest hardware store. His lungs burned with shallow breaths as he searched the streets from his position in the middle of the sidewalk. Someone had to have seen something. Anything. He needed—

"She's bleeding!" a girl said. "Someone call for an ambulance!"

The hairs on the back of his neck stood on end. Someone had been hurt? Pushing through the circle of onlookers, he caught sight of pink pajama pants and bright purple toenails. He surrendered to the panic as recognition flared. His heart threatened to burst straight out of his chest as he lunged for the unconscious six-year-old girl sprawled across the pavement. Pain shot through his knees as he scooped her into his arms. "Olivia!"

Don't miss
Midnight Abduction *by Nichole Severn,*
available June 2020 wherever
Harlequin Intrigue books and ebooks are sold.

Harlequin.com

HIEXP0520

Get 4 FREE REWARDS!

We'll send you 2 FREE Books
plus 2 FREE Mystery Gifts.

Harlequin Intrigue books are action-packed stories that will keep you on the edge of your seat. Solve the crime and deliver justice at all costs.

FREE
Value Over
$20
